PRAISE FOR *DUET FOR ONE*

"Martha Anne Toll's new novel is a beautiful meditation on love and the great vessel of time. Begin reading *Duet for One* to be stirred by its symphonic prose, and soon you'll harmonize and fall in love with its unforgettable characters."

—Jai Chakrabarti, author of *A Small Sacrifice for an Enormous Happiness* and *A Play for the End of the World*

"*Duet for One* is a lovely story about artistry, time, memory, and romance. Martha Anne Toll has a wonderful way of writing about music. It is a balm to the spirit!"

—Lydia Kiesling, author of *Mobility* and *The Golden State*

"Music—like love—is a challenge to both the senses and the intellectual mind. In this poignant and attentively written novel, Martha Anne Toll writes about the triumphs and sorrows of these two elements of human life, and considers how they might intertwine. *Duet for One* unfolds with symphonic sweep, each of its movements revealing deeper layers of emotion and insight into the central characters. The great works—works by Brahms, Beethoven, Schubert, Paganini, Mozart, Smetana— serve as the backdrop for Toll's clever and intricate storytelling. Truly, a memorable novel."

—Pauls Toutonghi, author of *The Refugee Ocean* and *Red Weather*

Also by Martha Anne Toll

Three Muses

Praise for Martha Anne Toll's *Three Muses*

"Exquisite"
—*The Washington Post*

"An intimate portrait of romance"
—NPR

"You're in the hands of a maestro"
—*New York Magazine*'s Vulture

"A deeply honest story"
—*POINTE Magazine*

"An affecting chamber piece"
—Starred *Kirkus Review*

DUET FOR ONE

Martha Anne Toll

Regal House Publishing

Published by
Regal House Publishing, LLC
Raleigh, NC 27605
All rights reserved

ISBN -13 (paperback): 9781646036004
ISBN -13 (epub): 9781646036011
Library of Congress Control Number: 2024944684

Cover images and design by © C. B. Royal

The following is a work of fiction created by the author. All names, individuals, characters, places, items, brands, events, etc. are either the product of the author's imagination or are used fictitiously. Any resemblance to actual events, places, institutions, persons, current or past, is entirely coincidental.

Excerpt from *An Equal Music* by Vikram Seth, copyright © 1999 by Vikram Seth. Used by permission of Broadway Books, an imprint of Random House, a division of Penguin Random House LLC. All rights reserved. Quote from *Edinburgh* by Alexander Chee, copyright © 2016, used by permission of the author. Quotations and ideas from *The Aesthetics of Survival*, copyright © 1984, 2004 by George Rochberg. Used by permission of the University of Michigan Press.

All efforts were made to determine the copyright holders and obtain their permissions in any circumstance where copyrighted material was used. The publisher apologizes if any errors were made during this process, or if any omissions occurred. If noted, please contact the publisher and all efforts will be made to incorporate permissions in future editions.

Regal House Publishing supports rights of free expression and the value of copyright. The purpose of copyright is to encourage the creation of artistic works that enrich and define culture.

Printed in the United States of America
Regal House Publishing, LLC
https://regalhousepublishing.com

In memory of
Max Aronoff (1906–1981)
Teacher, mentor, violist without peer

PART I

Music, such music is a sufficient gift. Why ask for happiness; why hope not to grieve? It is enough, it is to be blessed enough, to live from day to day and to hear such music—not too much, or the soul could not sustain it—from time to time.

—Vikram Seth, *An Equal Music*

1

October 2004

Adele Pearl was dead, vanquished by ovarian cancer. Adam and Victor shivered at her graveside. Adam was thirty-seven when his mother died. He was a violinist known for fluidity and grace.

Victor was Adam's father, the surviving half of Pearl and Pearl, a world-renowned two-piano team and joint piano faculty at Philadelphia's Caldwell Institute of Music.

Out of the corner of his eye, Adam watched Phillip Hissle hurry downhill. Hissle tripped, then bent to pick up his fedora from the damp, muddy ground. Instinctively, Adam moved closer to his father, although Hissle was too far away to create a disturbance.

For the small knot of mourners, time paused and music slept.

For Victor, Adele's death was a black hole that sucked in music.

For Adam, a numbness.

During those final weeks, Adam held vigil by Adele's hospital bed. Days stalled, lingered, and expanded. Adele's muscled pianist's fingers puffed up and went slack. Beeping monitors played tunes as Adam meandered backward in time.

He remembered sitting in Adele's lap at age four as she drilled the differences between black keys and white ones, her perfume as specific as her instruction. He heard the *tap, tap* of her heels down the marble hallway as she left for a performance. He recalled being seven, lying beneath his mother's piano, mesmerized by her golden soundboard, his ear pressed to the floor to feel her resonant bass, her left-hand notes cascading downward. Her right foot, beribboned in a black pump, hovered over the right pedal for the next decrescendo, while the hammers above Adam's head thumped like a marching band.

Growing up, Adam had wakened to Adele's practicing and gone to sleep to it. She was a severe taskmaster, harshest on herself. She thundered scales with a fierce dedication, two hands in parallel, two hands out from middle C and back again. Odysseys of departure followed by daredevil returns, a ravenousness that pushed her to the edge of sound; to be bigger, bolder, stronger; to puff wispy *pianissimos* and soar over rests.

Music critics were rhapsodic about Adele and Victor Pearl: *Pearl and Pearl created a rainbow of sound; Adele's yin to Victor's yang; recordings that sparkled with exquisite musicality.*

Adam, an only child, made them a family.

Two gravediggers winched Adele's casket into the dank earth. Mourners clustered around the gravesite, collars raised against the cold. Adam thought they were kind to come. Vladimir Rofsky, the pianist in Adam's trio, leaned on a walker after recent hip surgery. Dieter Brendt, his mother's favorite baritone, wiped a tearstained cheek with the back of his hand.

Victor was hunched and suddenly old.

Afterward, at home in his apartment, Victor sat mute in the green easy chair, his gaze lingering on the twin pianos at the far end of the living room. He offered a limp handshake to guests who murmured condolences, his silent nods a contrast to his customary warmth.

"As soon as Dad's up to it, we'll plan a memorial concert," Adam told the guests as he ushered them to the door.

Gradually, the hum in the apartment faded to silence. Victor rose to his feet.

"Anything I can do for you, Dad?" Adam asked.

"You can't bring her back," Victor said, shaking his head as he shuffled down the hall.

Adam cleared the living room, stacking cups and collecting trays of cold cuts, grateful that Phillip Hissle hadn't come over after the service. Phillip was on the viola faculty at Caldwell. He could be scornful.

Adam turned off the lights and got ready to leave. He was exhausted. His parents' pianos faced each other like beached whales. Someone had closed the lids and shut the keyboards.

Teary, wistful, Adam paused to ponder his parents' buttery harmonies, two pianos so much richer than one. Where did all that sound go?

He took the elevator down and stepped onto the sidewalk, relieved to be heading home. It was late. Philadelphia was shrouded in shadows and silence; no cars circled Rittenhouse Square. The shops were shuttered, restaurant lights out. Adam's shoes clicked audibly on the pavement.

What if his parents' music had traveled like light beams into the universe?

At his apartment, Adam hung his coat in the closet beside his concert tuxedo and a stack of neatly folded white shirts. The kitchen counters were clear, the dishes clean. Sheet music, books, and recordings lined the walls. Parquet floors ensured that when Adam practiced, the sound stayed live.

He sat on the edge of his bed, untied his shoes sprinkled with dirt from his mother's grave, and palmed his forehead where a well-placed kiss could have sent his headache packing. He raised his hands and stretched, torso flat as a teenage boy's. Unbuttoning his shirt, he gazed out at the city which sprawled beneath his bedroom window: colonial brick houses to the east, the Italian neighborhood to the south, and, farther away, the matte gray tankers dry-docked in the old Navy Yard.

In the hallway, a door slammed and the elevator shuddered.

Adam recalled standing in the doorway to the Pearls' apartment, a boy of eight or so, waiting for his parents to return from one of their endless tours. He would hold Bella's weathered hand and listen for the elevator. Bella, his Polish nanny, had a whiff of the old country about her. She was part grandmother and part nursemaid, gentle and devoted to Adam. She kept a pot of something tomatoey on the stove and served warm cookies after school.

The two would wait for an eternity, until the elevator grate squeaked open, and Victor and Adele stepped out, followed by the doorman lugging their trunks.

"How are you, my pumpkin?" Adele would hug Adam. "Has he been good?" she'd ask Bella. "Shall we give him the presents we brought?" Before Bella could respond, Adele released Adam and strode into their apartment. "What's for dinner? Are we square for tomorrow?"

Adam knew his mother was itching to get back to her piano. He would not be allowed to stay up for her stories. His mother would not say, "Adam, I'd much rather have been home with you, but I just had to go."

She was finally gone, who had been leaving him his whole life.

For company, Adam had his violin, a gleaming molasses-brown Guadagnini with ebony accessories.

He slid off its blue satin bag, pressed on a practice mute to avoid being heard, and walked to his music stand. A few stars twinkled in concert with the lights on the Ben Franklin Bridge. He opened the sheet music for the Bach sonatas and partitas.

Bare-chested, Adam played facing the expansive picture windows. His breathing was inseparable from the sweep of his right arm. He gave himself over to the music with the tenderness of a lover. Chords punctuated melody as haunting as death.

As he played, he recalled Dara, standing outside his practice room all those summers ago, listening to him play Bach. At the time, Adam had been playing to center himself—which had to do with Dara. Dara's listening in felt like an invitation—hers to him—despite her embarrassment at being caught.

Tonight he saw that he'd been too young for this music. A

lone violinist was soloist and accompanist, conductor and orchestra. Tonight the sonata erected scaffolding for grief.

Adam played into the night. He thought of Adele closing her eyes and leaning back on her piano bench—just for a moment—to complete a phrase. Sinking into her keyboard, fingers insistent yet gentle, she'd plumb musical depths, beads of sweat dotting her forehead. Her voice, tinkling on the telephone, punctuated by laughter, was authoritative when she oversaw young Adam's practicing or cajoled Victor during long rehearsals.

Sometimes Adam's parents had spent a week or more at home. When Adele wasn't practicing, she critiqued Adam's practicing, and when he was older, his performances. When she wasn't teaching, she enlisted his opinions on programming. When she wasn't traveling, she attended Adam's concerts and gave feedback—invited or not. Music had been their common language.

Dara sipped her coffee and glanced at the headline in the *Philadelphia Inquirer.* "Adele Pearl, Half of the Pearl and Pearl Two-Piano Team, Loses Battle with Cancer."

Impossible, Dara thought. Adele Pearl was immortal.

Dara gulped the rest of her coffee. This is what came from checking the paper first thing; you start the day with bad news and end up rushing.

Dara used to savor the morning. Matt would reach across the bed when she popped up at sunrise, give her a sleepy squeeze, or mutter a groggy "stay here" as he flopped his arm over her waist. She rarely stayed; mornings were too precious. She rose with an excited sense that time was hers alone, as if no one else in Philadelphia were awake. She greeted the day with bracing black coffee (Matt didn't do caffeine) and whatever novel was her current guilty pleasure. Professional reading, she'd decided, was off-limits at that hour.

Since Dara had left Matt, everything was different. Really,

Matt had left her, at least metaphorically. Dara had spotted him when she was on her way to the Free Library to chase down a reference. She'd caught him pressed against his secretary, Brittany—the one for whom Dara chose a yearly Christmas present, a pink wool pullover one year, a red-and-gold pashmina scarf the next. Brittany had graduated from high school two years earlier, and, according to Matt, was a crackerjack secretary. Apparently, she also had a pleasing rear. Matt's hand was placed possessively there, the same hand that stroked Dara in bed, that made her thrum. In fact, Brittany and Matt were as physically entwined as two people could be walking down a sidewalk.

Dara Kingsley's husband, Matthew Williams, Esquire, was cheating with the girl at work. Worse, Dara had been fond of Brittany. She was a go-getter, close to finishing her associate's degree, and had the smarts and drive to power through grad school. Now, it seemed, there was a reasonable chance she would do so as Mrs. Matthew Williams.

What misguided confidence she'd had in Matt, Dara reflected dismally. Her situation was so common, so tawdry, that if she'd read it in a student paper, she would have docked them a grade. She was left with revulsion (Matt's law partners must have known of his affair) and waves of self-reproach for her naiveté, which was catastrophic for her and immaterial to Matt.

Had Dara had a glimmer that underneath his hail-fellow-well-met charm, Matt was a worthless cur? Shame on her for not seeing it. And shame on her if she'd suppressed that perception in favor of a fantasy that had dumped her on the far side of marriage.

By now Dara had moved into her own place, two floors of a West Philadelphia row house, with heavy oak trim and a bay window facing Walnut Street. Despite the window, the apartment had scant natural light. Piles of unshelved books lay strewn around the living room. Cheap linoleum curled up at the corners of the kitchen floor. The cabinets and sinks had been fashionable circa 1959. But the place was blessedly hers.

She awoke each morning to an ugly replay of her gullibility, interspersed with cringing calculations about the mounting costs of her divorce. (Matt's partner represented him at no charge.)

Dara's class on the Victorian novel started early on Thursday mornings, but she couldn't leave the apartment without hearing Adam play. She turned on the New Philadelphia Trio's recording of Beethoven's "Archduke" and teared up as Adam's violin spiraled upward with the cello like a pair of honeysuckle vines. Dara's instrument was the viola, so this piece, scored for piano, violin, and cello, was one she'd never played. Maybe that was its appeal—harmonies spooled out in safe, neutral territory. Or perhaps it was being embraced in Adam's sound, or suspended in his rests—a frisson of hesitation before he made his entrance, as if he were tiptoeing into the room.

Sweet memories tangled with recollections that were like pinched nerves. Dara had left Adam abruptly, certain he'd have no trouble finding another girlfriend. Everyone loved Adam. It wasn't just his thick, dark hair and the way he dressed, in faded Levis and button-down cotton shirts. It was his depth. He was older than his years; there was seriousness in his brown eyes.

Dara had staved off remorse after their breakup. They'd had music in common, but only to a point. Adam had a gift and Dara did not.

Dara thought of her fifteen-year-old self, running up the steps to the Twenty-First Street Music School, swinging her viola case for her first lesson with Isaac Koroff.

She heaved open the massive oak door. Miss Irma Goodwin, the front office manager, pressed a buzzer. "Miss Kingsley has arrived," she announced into a speaker, her glasses tangled on a chain around her neck.

"Send her in!" Mr. Koroff bellowed.

Dara walked nervously into Mr. Koroff's studio. It felt like a museum. There was an ornate marble fireplace, dark wood trim, and Persian rugs on the floor. The walls were covered with old black-and-white photographs of musicians. Mr. Koroff's viola case lay open on a chair. His instrument shone in the late afternoon light.

Mr. Koroff seemed old, although he had a shock of brown hair. With his pipe between his teeth, he rose from behind a giant desk. He was a big man. He removed the pipe from his mouth and stirred the blackened tobacco with the tip of his index finger. "I'm a farmer," he joked as Dara stared at his dirty fingernails. "The missus and I have a weekend place in the Poconos. I love to dig around in dirt.

"So, you want to know about the pictures," he went on, although Dara hadn't said anything. "Franz Shochter," he said, pointing his pipe toward a photograph of a stern-looking violinist who looked like a cross between a 1940s movie star and Dracula. "Trained a generation of string players. And that there," he said, nodding toward a photo of four musicians, solemn in formal garb, instruments resting on their laps, "is the Caldwell String Quartet. Caldwell has free tuition for every student and attracts the best musicians in the world. But what about the musicians who aren't highfliers? The regular folks, the orchestra players of tomorrow? It's for them that I founded the Twenty-First Street Music School."

"Who's that?" Dara asked, emboldened by Mr. Koroff's informality. She pointed toward a photograph behind his desk of a middle-aged man in tweed bent over a viola student.

"Carl Taub, my teacher. He returned to Holland to give master classes during the War and was gassed by the Nazis. You recognize those two, I daresay?" With his pipe, Mr. Koroff gestured to a picture of two pianists smiling from their keyboards.

"Nope," Dara said, embarrassed.

"Victor and Adele Pearl, the best duo-piano team out there. Their son, Adam, is the concertmaster of the student orchestra here. If we can get you into shape, Miss Kingsley, you'll play in the orchestra too. Charles Jones is our conductor."

"The assistant conductor of the Philadelphia Orchestra!" Dara said. "I know who he is. My dad took me to the Philadelphia Orchestra children's concerts." She remembered the feel of the red velvet seats and Charles Jones's deep voice describing the music. He was famous!

"Very nice," Mr. Koroff said. "Enough chitchat, Miss Kingsley; take out your axe."

Dara unpacked her case as Mr. Koroff picked up his honey-colored viola. It had a scroll with a man's head carved into it and etched lines tracing its curves. "This beauty is Italian," he said. "Late 1700s. Mrs. Caldwell bought it for me. Well, for the school, I should say. But we have an understanding, she and I." He winked, a grin curving around the stump of his pipe. "You know about Mrs. Caldwell, do you, Miss Kingsley?"

"No," Dara said.

"She founded Caldwell. Rich as Croesus. The good lady once dug up four Stradivari for the Caldwell String Quartet to take on tour." He paused to relight his pipe, puffing on the stem until the tobacco smoldered red. His pipe had a man's face carved into it, just like the scroll on his viola. "We drove north to the Canadian border, where a customs officer asks us to post bond for the instruments. 'One hundred thousand dollars,' he says! So, I write him a check for a hundred grand. We do our tour. Our reviews were excellent, by the way. When we get back to the border, the customs official tears up the check." He leaned toward Dara, eyes twinkling. "I had twenty dollars in my checking account.

"Now let's get down to business." He lifted his viola to his chin, swept his bow in a circle, and alighted on the strings as if he were sinking into a marshmallow. His big, padded fingers bored into the fingerboard, rounding and deepening each note. "It's always and ever about tone," he instructed sternly. "Tone, tone, tone. I don't care if you're practicing by yourself or performing for the Queen of Sheba. You'll make it gorgeous, or you won't play at all. I hold my students to very high standards, Miss Kingsley," he continued, laying his viola back in its case. "And that means you."

Dara closed the *Philadelphia Inquirer* and finished her coffee.

How many string quartet performances had she attended? Listened to on the radio? In all that time she'd never heard a violist whose tone approached Isaac Koroff's. Violas were the beating heart of an orchestra's string section, the same for a string quartet. They were as indispensable for harmony as altos in a choir. Isaac's golden tone became her talisman.

The recording of Beethoven's "Archduke" was drawing to a close. Shaking off her reminiscences, Dara glanced at the kitchen clock—late for class. She grabbed the paper on her way out the door, once more scanning the obituary pages. *Funeral services are private. The Pearl family will announce a memorial concert at a later date.* What Pearl family? she wondered. There were only two left—Victor and Adam—unless Adam had married. Maybe he had kids.

Dara had preempted his leaving by leaving him first; she'd never believed his promises to stay with her. On the other hand, there was the look in his eyes when he saw her across the string section, the way his music spoke to her, and the memory of his arm, enveloping her like bark on a tree.

She wondered if she would go to a memorial concert. At the least, she could call Caldwell and get some information.

"Adam," Dara said, descending her front steps, as if they ever talked, or emailed, or anything else. "You gave me music."

She wasn't sure why, but she knew she wouldn't send a condolence note.

Adam had been playing for hours. Daylight was emerging, gray pushing away cobalt. He unscrewed his bow and slid a cotton handkerchief down the stick and under the fingerboard to clear away rosin dust. Then he tenderly dressed his violin in its blue satin bag.

He lay down on his bed, closed his eyes, and thought of Dara in the rear of the viola section. He could see her, even after all these years, her green eyes and thick chestnut braid, her small breasts outlined by a black cardigan. She had no interest in fashion. She wore faded brown corduroy pants that were several sizes too large. She arrived at rehearsals lugging a backpack stuffed with books, her hands smeared in blue ballpoint ink, with a pencil stuck through her braid for marking the music. For concerts, she wore a floor-length black skirt over a scoop-necked leotard, nothing like the frilly blouses other girls wore. The way she embraced her viola—left hand in classic Isaac Koroff position, bow arm circling downward—made Adam want to transform into a genie and hide inside it.

He'd heard she'd married and was an English professor at Penn.

What about the intervening years? Adam had been with other women, of course. Fine musicians, every one. What about Patti?

Adam was sinking to the bottom of love's ocean, layers of pressure bearing down. He may as well be twenty-one again, he loved Dara that much tonight—or was it already tomorrow? He pictured Dara lying on his twin bed as she turned pages in a textbook while he practiced, saturating the room with sound. Her presence was reassuring. Comforting.

"Dara," Adam said to no one in particular, "my mother died."

2

Adam zipped his jacket and walked past Boathouse Row. It was a cold morning. The Philadelphia Museum of Art, a copy of the Parthenon overlooking the Schuylkill River, was awash in pink. His walk lent him a sliver of hope, as if autumn had been deferred. Sculling boats skimmed the river, oars dipping in and out, evoking a Thomas Eakins painting.

He was glad he'd invited Patti Lee for dinner tonight; he'd begun to miss her. He hadn't slept with her since his mother lapsed into her final coma.

Patti came from Seoul to study with Adele at Caldwell and stayed. Before Patti, Adam had never been involved with one of his parents' students. Before Patti, Adam had never been involved with a pianist. He wasn't sure whether he and Patti were still a couple, or whether they ever had been. Well, he'd make dinner for her and open a bottle of wine and they would see.

He headed east on the Parkway toward the Reading Terminal Market. The Amish butcher was reeling up his awning, but Adam thought Patti would prefer fish. Adam walked down the aisle to Philadelphia Seafood, where two men in rubber boots were dumping buckets of crushed ice into dented metal display bins. "Is it too early to buy a filet?"

"I was awake before you were born," the man behind the counter said. He might not have shaved since then either. "How much you need?" He slapped a large flounder onto the board. Steadying it under his thick fingers, he cut translucent slices too quickly for Adam to see his knife strokes.

Adam maneuvered through a crowd at the bakery and got behind the line of workers buying muffins for the office. "Breakfast?" the woman in a white apron teased as she boxed up his small raspberry pie.

Adam smiled. "No, it's dessert."

As she secured a string around the box, the woman added, "Must be for a lady friend."

Adam couldn't contain his embarrassment. He wanted to tell her that he kept things light with Patti, but that Patti understood; she was a grown-up.

On the way home, Adam detoured to Nineteenth Street to pick up violin strings. Pulling open the door to Moennig's, Adam was greeted with a tangy varnish smell. He liked the old-world feel of the shop, stringed instruments hanging from the walls. In the rear he saw old Mr. Moennig's son, Billy, bent over a cello, his ear to the f-hole.

Adam and Billy had played in the same recital when they were fourteen, both studying in the Caldwell Preparatory Division. Adam played Beethoven's "Spring Sonata." In the buzz of audience members milling around the Caldwell Common Room during the reception, Adam's father came up and said, "Violinists twice your age would sell their souls to produce a sound like yours. Melodies melt like butter in your hands. You're lucky, son."

Adam's teacher, Yuri Zablonsky, arrived just then. "Nice job." He was a tall, white-haired man, slightly stooped. He grinned at Adam. "And your mother did a nice job accompanying you."

"We'll overlook the B natural in the Scherzo," Adele said, joining them.

"We will indeed," Yuri said, putting his arm around Adam, who was mortified. He looked around to see if anyone else had heard. Probably the whole room. His mother was using her loud company voice.

"Is Billy Moennig one of your students?" Adele asked Yuri. Yuri nodded.

"He did an excellent job!"

Adam slipped off for a glass of lemonade. Why hadn't his mother waited until they were outside? He knew he'd missed that B flat. He stepped into the damask draperies to hide and stared up at Mrs. Caldwell, who surveyed the room from her oil portrait, hands folded across her lap. With her pursed lips, crown of silver hair, and light-blue gown, she looked scary.

Why was his mother nicer to Billy than to him? Yuri and Victor hadn't mentioned Adam's mistake, while Adele seemed pleased that Billy had played better. Adam knew his mother dropped notes in performances, but he also knew not to mention it. She would have puffed up and gotten angry or, worse, sulked.

"Mistakes are inevitable, Adam," Adele said on the way out of Caldwell. "You can't learn any other way. Lots of mistakes come from nerves. You need nerves to stay focused, but there can be too much of a good thing too!"

"We all make mistakes," Victor added, a little too eagerly.

"I know, I know," Adam said irritably. "You don't have to say anything."

"Adam." Adele stopped in front of their apartment building and faced her fourteen-year-old son, hands on his shoulders. "The important thing is work—there is no substitute. You've got to be prepared. All the talent in the world is worthless without the labor."

"You've mentioned that before."

"But there's something else," she said. "You know when I make the most mistakes?"

"No, Mother, I don't."

"When I've had liftoff, when I get so absorbed that I go over the edge and just let it fly. That's when I tend to drop notes."

"That's a good thing, Adele," Victor said, looking at Adam out of the corner of his eye. "Giving the full range of your emotions to the music."

"Quite," Adele said.

"How's your father?" Mr. Moennig asked Adam from behind the glass counter, a hint of Austria in his speech.

"I wish I knew," Adam said, setting his raspberry pie box on the counter. When had Adam's father played a concert without his mother? Or done anything without her? Adam ached the way a rainy day recalls a broken bone. "As well as can be expected," Adam said. "I guess." Adele had been the one who convinced agents about the possibilities of representing a two-piano team, who badgered the Caldwell librarian to come up with pieces to perform and doggedly pursued new concert venues.

"I'm sorry I missed the funeral," Mr. Moennig said.

"We kept it small," Adam said. "We're trying to figure out some kind of memorial concert in her honor."

"What a team, your parents," Mr. Moennig said.

"Yes," Adam said. "Opposites attract."

He paid for his strings and left.

Crossing Rittenhouse Square, Adam recalled his mother's remarks at that childhood recital with as much confusion as when he was a boy. She could be like that—bitingly critical, then at the last moment, drop a nugget that you needed. Emotionally engaged performances mattered. If you got ahead of your fingers, it wasn't the end of the world. People went to concerts to hear humans, not machines.

Adam adjusted the pie box in his hand and pulled open the door to his building, remembering the boy in his sixth-grade class pelting him with mud, shouting, "Look at that faggy case! Balling around with your violin!" Adam hadn't made it to his lesson at Caldwell that day; he went straight home.

"Let's take this off," Bella said, helping him with his sweater. "We'll scrub the pants too. Go change, and I'll get you cleaned up."

Adele came to the bathroom door and watched Bella rinse Adam's cheeks. "That boy's just a mean kid with nothing better to do," Adele said. The water was cold on Adam's face. "He can't hurt you," she added, heading back to her piano.

Bella handed Adam a towel. He decided that when he was dry, he'd lie under his mother's piano and fill his head with rumblings from her soundboard. If he closed his eyes, the floor would hum.

Adele had other plans. She called from the living room. "Adam, take out your violin. This is Rachmaninoff's *Vocalise,*" she said, waving a piece of music. "Originally for soprano, even though it doesn't have lyrics. A song without words. Some people think it's meant to be heard in a dentist's chair, but I think it's beautiful. Play it with me, son. This will be your lesson." Adam knew he wasn't allowed to decline.

The piece was pretty. It took concentration to ensure he had enough bow to draw out the long phrases. Adam's head filled with wavy melody and melancholy harmonies. As they completed the final ritard, his mother's face glowed. She looked up from her piano bench and smiled. "I knew you'd feel better," she said. And the funny thing was, he did.

Later that afternoon, his parents had a fight with Adam sitting right there in the kitchen. "What happened when you called the school?" Victor said.

"I figured you'd do it."

"Jesus!" Victor grabbed the phone. Raking his hand through his tight graying curls, he demanded to speak to the principal. He slammed the receiver down and turned to Adele. "Was that so hard?"

"He loved *Vocalise*, didn't you, son?" Adele said.

Adam gave a cautious nod, unsure whose side to be on, or even what they were fighting about.

"It calmed him down," Adele said. "By the way, Sid Gellman is coming at nine tomorrow to tune the pianos." She swept out of the kitchen.

Victor stormed after her.

"You have no problem calling Sid," Victor shouted, without a trace of his usual refinement. "No problem chatting it up when he gets here," he snarled at Adele. "How come talking to regular people scares you? You're the boy's mother, for God's sake!"

Adam didn't like being spoken of as if he weren't there. And he did not want to be a boy who couldn't stand on his own two feet at school.

3

The fish is excellent," Patti said. "Now tell me about the trio." Patti's black hair was clipped behind her head, wisps falling down the sides. Her hands were smooth. Her fingers had a stubbiness that belied their elasticity on the keyboard.

"Thanks for helping out," Adam said. He felt uncomfortable that he'd asked her to substitute for Vladimir Rofsky, who was recovering from hip surgery, but his discomfort wasn't with Patti's playing. She was a reliable pianist.

Adam slipped off his shoe and ran his foot up Patti's stockings.

"Adam!"

"Vladimir's going to take a while to recover," Adam said.

"I've learned most of the Mendelssohn, and I'm still getting through the Dvořák. I need to soften it up," she said as Adam moved his foot farther up the inside of her leg. "I don't want it to sound clunky. How long have you three been together?"

"My family? I guess since I was born."

"I was asking about your trio."

Right. Patti wouldn't be asking about his family. Was he in this conversation, even in this room? "Ten years, maybe a little longer. We've never played with another pianist."

"You don't have a choice, with Vladimir out."

"You'll do a great job," Adam said, picking up her hand across the table.

"Two of my students are preparing their Juilliard auditions, two trying for Indiana University," she said.

Adam pushed back his chair and walked around the table.

"I'm overscheduled," Patti said. "My hands are full."

Adam stood behind her. "I'd like to have my hands full," he

said, running his palms over her breasts. "Come," he suggested, bending down to kiss her ear.

"We'll clean up first." Patti got up to clear the table. "I'll wash the dishes; you cooked."

Holding up a small hand in a rubber glove covered in suds, Patti said, "How did your mother do it? My hands are the same size. Her *fortes* were so powerful."

Patti's parents were healthy and young, half a world away. Maybe that's why she was so matter of fact. Adam didn't really want her asking how he was doing anyway. No one asked how he was doing—not Patti, not Mr. Moennig. Maybe it was better that way. Maybe grief, if that's what this fuzzy haze was, was meant to be private. In public, Adam was supposed to be on top of things. "Did you ever notice that the higher up you are, the straighter the lines?" he asked.

Patti turned around, puzzled.

"From an airplane, the roads look straight. Think of my parents," Adam said. "The contours of their relationship seem smooth. The further away you are. Inside the family," he continued, "the less smooth are the lines."

"No turbulence, no banging, so much internal force," Patti said. "It must have been something to have Adele for a mother. Especially when you're young. To have that kind of musician right in the house."

Adam smiled. "If you like boot camp."

"I was so nervous for my first lesson at Caldwell that I had a memory lapse in the middle of my Chopin *Mazurka*," Patti said. "I'd performed it in Seoul, no problem. Got here and forgot. Your mother said, 'Let's have a cup of tea.' You know that electric pot she used to keep in her studio? This was the middle of the lesson. She said, 'Patti, tell me about your family. Do you have brothers and sisters? What's the weather like there now?' I forgot about the piece. After we finished tea, your mother said, 'Try it again, Patti.' It went fine. Everything came back. Your mother was so kind."

Adam knew his mother was beloved by her students. They

were fiercely loyal to her, sending her updates from around the world. No matter her concert schedule, Adele responded to every email and answered every letter. Her students sought advice while lauding the rock-solid technique she'd taught them. Every finger a distinct instrument, the right hand largely responsible for melody, the left in charge of harmony and bass and rhythm—but not always and not necessarily. Together, a rich ensemble.

There were strict rules, but they were made to be broken. Each composer was unique, each piece an independent work of art. It was the pianist's duty to interpret the notes on a page with clarity and utmost respect for the composer.

Adele gave her students a winning combination. She taught them to phrase, to strike the exquisite balance between right hand and left, to wring the music's quintessence with shimmering melodies and polished harmonies, while insisting on athletic technique. She was as acclaimed a teacher as she was a performer.

Adam appreciated his mother's teaching. He'd encountered any number of automatons: instrumentalists with stratospheric technique who lacked musicianship. Adele developed well-rounded students, musicians with the power to withstand the pressure and limelight of solo careers, but for whom chamber music came as naturally as breathing. Small wonder she was beloved.

Patti set the last dish in the drainboard and dried her hands. She walked over to her purse and took out some hand cream. "Okay," she said, rubbing in the lotion. She gave Adam a sideways glance and moved toward his bed. Kicking off her pumps, she lay down. Adam sat beside her and stroked her side—her sweater, the businesslike wool skirt, her nylons.

She gazed at him and smiled. "Sorry I can't stay tonight. Too much to do in the morning."

"Let's take these off," he said, finding the clasp to her pearls.

"Lots of clothing; I had to teach before I came over." She didn't seem inclined to help.

Naked, she turned sideways, her hair cascading down her spine. He was stimulated by her languor, by her almost imperceptible response to his touch. She was relaxed, even diffident. He could feel her nipple hardening under his index finger, but her breathing sounded as if she were asleep. He tipped her toward him and gripped her shoulders.

When it was over, he wished he'd gone slower. "Are you sure you can't stay?"

She shook her head.

"I'll take you home."

They walked arm in arm toward Delancey Street. At her door Patti said, "Come over Thursday?"

"Can I let you know? I have a student playing a recital that night, and I'm going to try to bring my father. I need to get him moving." Adam kissed her lightly on the lips and turned to go.

The biting air felt good. He walked back to Rittenhouse Square and sat on a bench. The park was empty except for two men sharing a bottle from a paper bag. Something had struck them silly.

It was after midnight, but Adam had no interest in going to bed. He stared at the bare tree branch overhead to see if he could find where the sound of mourning doves was coming from. Billy, the bronze billy-goat statue, iconic in Rittenhouse Square, looked bereft—no children climbing on him or rubbing his head to make his patina shine. Adam felt disembodied, blurred. He wondered if he was in shock, then dismissed the idea. But he couldn't remember what he had to do tomorrow and wasn't sure what he'd done yesterday.

When he returned home, the raspberry pie was sitting on the counter, the box unopened.

4

Time for Otakar Ševčík," Isaac said to Dara at her fourth lesson. "He's been ambushing string players for decades. If you plow through, you'll be able to make your way around your axe, guaranteed. Got your notebook?" Isaac picked up a sharpened pencil and wrote - -- - -- - --.

"Da *dum* da *dum* da *dum*. Invert. Then we'll embellish. First finger holds its place while second pounds like a piston. Your left hand must have the strength of a football player!" He retrieved a plastic model of a hand from his oak desk. "Doctors have nothing on us," he said, lifting off the top of the model and pointing at the musculature inside. "The tendon for your third finger is underneath your second. So, work that third finger extra hard."

Dara's left hand was flimsy. In her right hand, the bow slid over the strings.

Isaac lit his pipe. "Play like an oboist. We don't hear them breathe. I had to beat down the door to study with Marcel Tabuteau at Caldwell, even though I played viola and he was an oboist. Ever heard of him?"

"Nope."

"His students sat in front of a candle, blowing steadily so the flame turned blue but never went out." Mr. Koroff set his pencil on the heavy black music stand. "I'm talking about your bow arm. Keep that candle burning blue. No break in tone when you change the direction. The bow is the viola's lungs."

For her bow arm, endless circles. Her right shoulder ached and her arm tired.

"I expect you to practice three hours a day at least. If you don't treat each note as if it were part of your Carnegie Hall debut, you're wasting your time." He looked at her tearing eyes. "You'll get the hang of it.

"I coach a quartet of old ladies," he said, smiling. "Two of them gave the Twenty-First Street School money. One day I come in and they're happily sawing away, but something sounds off. Three of them are playing Mozart, and the other one's playing Haydn. Focus on what you're doing and don't be an old lady! I'm from Missouri, the 'Show-Me State.' Show me that luscious sound!"

The sound of Mr. Koroff's finger hitting the fingerboard was like a woodpecker tapping. His tone was fat and expressive, unutterably beautiful.

"Out of tune! Open those ears! What are they there for? You have *two* of them!"

To Dara's quivering lip, "You're the ninety percent," he said. "The teacher can only give ten percent. You do the work."

Dara's fingers calloused. She kept a nail clipper in her viola case so her nails didn't impede her practicing.

At school, Dara looked at her hands and saw they were changing. Her knuckles stuck out more; the fleshy part on the side of her left hand was hardening. She was right-handed, but her left hand was becoming stronger than her right.

She was getting better, and she knew it. Her shoulders were no longer sore after practicing three hours. She focused on each note, became more discerning. Pieces that were once out of reach now seemed possible.

Her father would come home from work and listen to her toiling away. "Don't you get tired of playing one note?" He teased her—lovingly—but she knew what she was after: finding the magic of Isaac's tone.

Every few days she was intoxicated with a smooth, scratchless down-bow that began in her stomach and filled up her head.

5

Victor laid his wife's obituary on her piano like a funeral wreath. He should paste it into her concert album; it would be the final entry.

CELEBRATED DUO-PIANIST DIES
Adele Pearl, renowned for virtuosity and sensitivity at the keyboard, succumbed to ovarian cancer yesterday. She was a member of a duo-piano team, her husband Victor Pearl comprising the other half...

Half a duo was no duo at all, the right hand of a piano concerto, the bottom line of a piano sonata.

Adele was as meticulous about chronicling her life as she had been about learning music, but Victor hadn't paid attention to her scrapbooks.

What else did he have to do now? He took one off the shelf, leafed through, and found the yellowed programs from Vienna and Paris, where they'd traveled when Adam was an infant. A picture of Victor and Adele, hands on their piano lids, accepting bouquets of flowers at the Musikverein. Their next set of concerts were in New England (Boston, Portsmouth, Portland), shortly after they returned home.

The following pages featured baby Adam—learning to sit, smiling at the camera as he crawled. Adorable in a red jumpsuit, out for a stroll around Rittenhouse Square, his tiny hand in Adele's. "I don't remember taking that," Victor said to the empty room, but he must have. Adele had annotated each of the photos in her confident hand, dating them with precision, the same as she had done with Pearl and Pearl's tour pictures.

He closed the cover of the scrapbook, wondering at his surprise. Why wouldn't she have given Adam equal prominence to their concerts?

Victor heard Adam's key in the door and watched Phillip Hissle limp in behind. "You met her at Aspen?" Adam was asking. Nodding toward Victor, Hissle handed Adam his fedora. Without the hat, Hissle's silver hair shone brighter.

"Adele was a great woman," Hissle said. He spoke quietly; Victor had trouble hearing him. "My condolences, Victor."

"We met Phillip the summer we played Brahms's *Liebeslieder Waltzes*," Victor said dreamily from his green easy chair. Hissle walked over and took the matching chair, a teak end table between them.

"The mountains in Aspen were covered with purple and yellow columbine," Victor said. "Cool, clean air." He turned to Adam. "Your mother was in the early months of her pregnancy."

Like plants and children, Pearl and Pearl had had their musical growth during summers. Victor wished his son would go to summer festivals. He would meet more artists, see the country. Get out of himself, which he sorely needed.

"No," Hissle said, disrupting Victor's reverie. "I knew Adele before I knew you, Victor."

"Ah," said Victor. "How could I have forgotten?"

"I didn't realize he was so fond of you, Dad," Adam said, closing the door behind Hissle.

"He's not. It's your mother, though he had a funny way of expressing it. Never a kind word. Hissle sidled up to your mother after our *Liebeslieder* performance and said something like, 'I doubt you meant to drown out the singers. You should have lowered the piano lids all the way.' As if we hadn't thought of that! As if we were imbeciles! I'd never even met him."

"She must have been furious," Adam said.

"I think the Karminsky Quartet had just hired him. I said, 'Hissle has some nerve, and right after a concert.'"

"'I think it was gutsy of him.' That's what your mother said. I remember it like yesterday. 'Gutsy'? Hissle was downright rude." Victor glared at the two pianos and imagined heaving them out the window. "I never cared for Hissle's playing," Victor said. "Remember that review in the *Times*? 'What Mr. Hissle lacks in technique, he makes up in bombast.' Glad they never said that about us."

Adam laughed.

"Hissle was at the funeral," Adam said. "Sprained his ankle running down the hill."

"Really? Says something about your mother."

"What?" Adam asked.

"Or Hissle," Victor said. He closed his eyes to summon fresh air and mountain breezes. Seeing his radiant wife across the lid of his piano in Aspen, Victor was as lovestruck as a schoolboy. Brahms's Ländlers pinged around his brain, music lost to time.

"I have a student giving a recital tonight," Adam said, kneeling next to Victor's easy chair. "Alice Chang. You're coming, Dad; she's playing the Franck Sonata."

Victor groaned. He couldn't sit through that sonata. Adam was usually considerate, but this request was tin-eared.

"Dad, you have to get out. And you and I have to start planning Mother's memorial concert."

"Have I told you about the first time I heard your mother play?"

"Have you given her memorial any thought?"

"We were at Tanglewood that summer," Victor said. "Your mother was Adele Hammond then. She was nineteen and looked like a Main Line debutante. Strawberry blond, petite, dressed in cashmere sweater sets and her 'good luck' coral necklace. I thought she'd blow over at the first wind. I almost missed her concert because I had work to do! I'm still not sure why I went."

He shuddered, appalled that he could have ended up with that Viennese girl his mother had chosen. Victor was the lone child of Viennese refugees. His parents had left everything behind and settled in Washington Heights.

Victor was a tall man, well over six feet. He could have

played college basketball but had been flagged early as a piano prodigy. His mother, proud and imperious, had navigated the New York musical establishment to obtain the best instruction, imparting her old-world politesse to Victor.

If he had married that young woman his mother chose for him, Victor would have become a collectible, an item to trot out and display. Would have wilted and ended up a community music teacher in some two-bit American suburb. Or become the opposite, with lovers strewn across the world, bedding them when he touched down for a day or two to perform. It would have been exhausting. And lonely.

"I remember your mother's dress," Victor said to Adam, who was edging toward the door. "Sleeveless gray satin. You've seen the picture." Victor motioned toward the living room shelf—a black-and-white photograph of Adele, hardly more than a girl. "By the way, Adam, speaking of pictures. It turns out your mother's albums are filled with pictures of you. I thought they were just for our concerts."

"Dad...we have to go."

"You'll be interested that she filled those scrapbooks with you."

"I'll take a look," Adam said, sounding like he had no such intention.

"At the concert, Giorgio Petroni had top billing," Victor continued, standing up. "Solid violinist. Not as good as you. He went back to Rome after that summer. He's still concertmaster of the opera orchestra there. He and Adele opened the program with the *Franck Sonata in A Major.*

"She was so powerful." Victor sat back down, inhabiting his younger self, hearing Adele for the first time. "Centered, direct-ed, her playing commanding and lyrical. The music emanated from her and not the piano... I rushed backstage at intermission," Victor said, reliving his frustration. Standing taller than the tight-knit group crowding in on her, Victor could see her but couldn't get near. "The next morning, she was at break-fast. I introduced myself and tried to compliment her playing.

She wasn't interested." Victor had been crushed; without even knowing her, he'd missed his chance.

"Dad, let's go. I've heard this story once or twice or a hundred times."

Adam wasn't giving up. "I'm too tired to put up a fight," Victor said, walking toward the hall closet. Adam helped him with his camel hair coat.

"I see you've polished your wingtips and got your white silk scarf," Adam said, with affected cheer.

Victor took his son's arm, and they walked the two blocks to Caldwell.

"You were engaged the next time you met Mother," Adam said, trying for conciliation.

Victor appreciated the prompt. "My mother had chosen her. Can you imagine your mother finding a girl for you to marry?"

"No way."

"Your grandmother was furious when I broke the engagement. Took her years to get over it." They waited for the light at Eighteenth and Locust to turn green.

"The next time I met your mother," Victor said, "she found me. We were both teaching at Tanglewood. She knocked on my office door and said she wanted to play a two-piano concert. Approached me with a stack of music—Mozart, Brahms, Poulenc. Sat down at my keyboard and sounded out melodies as if she valued my input."

"She knew how to get what she wanted."

"She asked if I remembered her," Victor continued. "After that sublime Franck Sonata! Said she wished she had come to my Carnegie Hall debut."

"Wasn't that unusual?" Adam said. "For her to focus on someone beside herself?"

Victor ignored the comment. He longed to convince his son that Adele was better, so much better, than Adam's judgment of her, but he was too tired to take that on right now. Or take on anything else, for that matter. He wished he hadn't come out tonight. He sighed and pushed on. "Your mother liked that the reviewer said I played like a 'consummate chamber musician.' She never wanted to bang out warhorses with orchestras."

Victor untied and reknotted his scarf. "Your mother was a magnificent pianist." Victor had never wavered from that view. He had a simple appreciation of Adele's talent, unencumbered by the jealousy that rankled many musical relationships. Perhaps it was because of his accidental first hearing of her playing, or because he had never loved anyone the way he loved her. Or maybe it had to do with the extraordinary power contained in those small hands. Or with her control over the instrument. Adele never let her strength overtake her musicality. She pulled music out of every note like a famine victim sucking marrow. Her practicing was rigorous and deliberate, yet she exuded spontaneity in performance.

Or maybe it was Adele's raw adoration of her work, the passion that had overcome obstacles big and small to make them Pearl and Pearl. Like the time Victor left one of his concert shoes behind in Bordeaux and didn't discover it until an hour before their concert in Lyons. The shops were already closed. Adele located a can of black paint backstage and painted his sock to match.

Or the incredulous looks they got from agents, who were convinced that two-piano teams wouldn't sell. In the end, Adele faced down the San Francisco–based Herman Stickman on one of his rare visits to Philadelphia and insisted he book them. Stickman had represented them ever since.

"I wish you had someone in your life—a partner—who provided that kind of boost," Victor said to Adam.

Adam looked at him. "Dad, please." They climbed the marble steps to the Caldwell Institute of Music.

Caldwell Hall was intimate, an oversized living room of a nineteenth-century mansion, paneled in fruitwood. It was nearly full when they arrived. Adam seated his father and went to greet his students. As Victor removed his overcoat, concert-goers left their seats to pay their respects. Victor was forced into conversation, even to smile. A few students asked when he planned to resume teaching. "Next week." He surprised himself. "I'll be back next week."

The lights dimmed. Alice Chang and her accompanist walked onstage. The music of César Franck spilled into the room. Alice had a silken sound, typical of Adam's students. Adam could play and he could teach. He taught an astounding number of students to imitate his sound.

Victor was sad for his son. His mother was dead, and instead of mourning, Adam was mired in resentment. Adele was so much more than the taskmaster Adam understood her to be. Victor hoped hostility wouldn't drag his son down.

How could Adele be gone? Each time Victor got near that reality, it was an electric shock. He had watched her take her last breath, but he would never, ever get used to it.

Concertgoers in Caldwell Hall cleared their throats as Alice tuned up for the second movement of the Franck. Victor saw Adam smiling at him from the wings. What a good son. Victor could see Adele in Adam's face—her eyes, her smile.

Victor had never told the rest of his story to Adam; it was too private. Victor and Adele, discovering one another. Victor's playing had a darker, deeper sound, Adele's a counterbalance with its singing tone. When their third rehearsal finished at midnight, Victor suggested a walk around the Tanglewood grounds. Adele hooked her arm in his and asked whether they might repeat their upcoming concert that fall in New York.

"I'm getting married in October," Victor said unexpectedly.

"That doesn't answer whether you want to repeat this concert."

"My mother thinks it's a good idea."

"The marriage or the concert?"

"The marriage."

Adele stopped to look up at him. "What do you think?"

"I think the woman I should marry is standing in front of me right now."

"I'm glad you've given it so much thought."

Victor flushed with the memory. Adele waited outside while he went for a blanket. Holding her close, he guided her across the grounds, carried her over a creek, and walked with her into the woods at the edge of the Tanglewood property.

It was a warm July night. They already knew what they shared in music. During the night, they created a vision for a joint future—playing and loving, at home and at work. Their bodies, their fingers and hands, their rapt ears. When the sun rose, they had become two people with one dream.

They were meant to be. Victor had known that as much as he'd ever known anything.

The third movement of the sonata began. A dramatic piano opening, followed by a short violin cadenza.

Victor thought of the contrasts that made Adele. How she would stand over a student and deliver a pointed critique of their fingering, followed by a reassuring hug at the end of the lesson. Her shouting at top volume for Victor to play *pianissimo* when they practiced. Her fierce loyalty. The way she worked the Green Room after a concert: clasping audience members' hands between hers, drinking in compliments. Not releasing her grip until she'd heard about their children and careers. Her effervescent personality masked an iron will and an uncompromising attention to detail.

Adam was right; Victor needed to focus on Adele's memorial concert. Victor wanted to honor his wife's memory. So many people eager to come, so many musicians clamoring to play. It should be here in Caldwell Hall, filled with her students. He and Adam could play the Franck Sonata. Victor tapped his fingers in tandem with Alice's accompanist. Adam would shine in this third movement, with its *recitativo* passages. He would be all over the fingerboard, making those passages appear effortless.

Victor and Adele made the music for their wedding. It was a small affair; Victor's mother had been too angry to come. Adele's piano teacher generously gave over his apartment for the occasion. He owned two Bösendorfers ("not one, but *two!*" Adele had exclaimed). The tiny group of guests stood during the afternoon ceremony, before breaking out their instruments to make music into the night.

Victor had played at his own wedding; couldn't he play at his wife's memorial? Didn't he owe her that much? A tear dripped down his cheek.

Caldwell Hall filled with applause. Victor had missed the fourth movement of the Franck. No matter. The movement was part of his unconscious; hearing it was like returning home. So easy to sing, a jubilant culmination to the sonata.

At the very least, he and Adam would close the program with the Franck Sonata, and Adele could smile down on them.

6

R ests are the key to the music." Isaac's face was inches away from Dara's. "Music captures time; it molds and bends it. Sound *is* the passage of time."

"That's cool," Dara said.

"There is no music without silence." Isaac plowed ahead. "Rests define time. Your bow arm is responsible for rests. If you're lazy or imprecise, you'll ruin the energy. Watch!" He raised his voice, startling her. "We're flicking at the frog." He gripped his instrument with his chin and pointed with his left hand to the mother-of-pearl base of his bow, the frog, where he'd placed his fingers. "First, my nose." Bow in hand, he curved his right wrist and touched the end of his aquiline nose. "Repeat ten times. No wiggling; hold the tip steady."

By the tenth time, the tip of Dara's bow had stopped moving.

"Let's go!" Isaac touched the bow hair nearest the frog to his string and, with a *ping*, lifted it. "Reverse!" He pinged in the opposite direction. Using less than an inch of bow hair, his pings popped like bubbles.

Grinning, Isaac waved his bow at the ceiling. "Now for the tip."

The tip was harder, Dara found. The bow's weight made it difficult to land.

"Brush your bow as if you were a ballerina brushing her feet against the floor! Time to ping and flick." Eyes closed, he pinged and flicked with the exactitude of a snare drummer, while Dara's bow bounced around her strings like an errant tennis ball.

❧

Adam couldn't come up with a reason not to go to Patti's after Alice Chang's recital. He dropped his father off and walked down Delancey Street past the brightly colored doors that shone beneath the street lamps.

Patti lived in a basement apartment. As he approached, Adam heard her practicing the Mendelssohn trio they were about to start rehearsing. She sounded good, with a nice attack on the keys and well-rounded *pianissimos*.

It was a cold night, but he didn't want to interrupt her. She wouldn't have let him anyway. He paced the sidewalk outside her door. He could hear her tendency to rush. If she did that in rehearsal, he'd have to say something. He recalled Victor's right foot thump-thumping on the floor as Adam lay under his mother's soundboard, his father simultaneously trying to slow Adele down while maintaining a steady rhythm.

Why did Adam's every thought culminate with his mother?

Adele hadn't been like other parents, who sweated the details of their children's lives, who asked about friends or worried when assignments were due. Adam felt out of place when his classmates complained they couldn't watch TV until they'd finished their homework. His family had never owned a TV, and his mother paid no attention to homework. If Adele was home, she was working.

Adam disliked the version of himself who'd emerged in the shadow of his mother's death. He was supposed to feel sad and mournful; instead, he felt like he had a rash that itched all over. Tetchy and irritable, he descended the three steps to Patti's.

Dara practiced like a demon and arrived at her next lesson ready to ping and flick with confidence.

Isaac was delighted. "You're the ninety percent; the teacher can only be ten percent. You're doing damn well, Miss Kingsley. You're ready for our orchestra now."

Dara grinned. To play under the great Charles Jones? At age sixteen, she had been handed a miracle.

It pleased Adam that Patti preferred for him to undress her.

Even at home, she rarely dressed casually. Tonight she wore a merino pullover, a herringbone skirt, and stockings with black pumps. When he lifted her sweater and unzipped her skirt, she stood in a slip. He liked the way she shivered when he fingered her through the gauzy fabric.

Patti was willing and relaxed. It took an effort for him to ensure that she was pleasured, that her half smile suggested something other than a day well spent. On top of her, Adam wished she would hold him tighter, that she would indicate more than simple desire. A need for him, maybe, that stretched beyond companionable lovemaking.

Maybe it was he who was in need. For what?

As he lay with Patti, his mind floated to Dara, how they used to lie facing each other in his twin bed. It was so narrow, she had to lie up against him. He would press his face to her breasts and draw her to him, a hand at the small of her back.

What was wrong with him?

"Adam, it's time to move in together," Patti said. "Your place is too small for my piano, and my place is too small for you. We'll have to find a new place."

Adam was alarmed, and discomfited by both his alarm and Patti's businesslike tone. And with the understanding that she had every right to ask this of him.

Yesterday Adam had coached his Caldwell chamber students in Bedřich Smetana's quartet "From My Life." The quartet was Smetana's admission that the whistling in his ear indicated his oncoming deafness. In the final movement, Smetana wrote a high-pitched squeal into the first violin part. No matter how many times Adam heard it, that squeal shocked.

He looked at Patti and skimmed his hand down her shoulder to her forearm. Her question jarred; it was too future facing. It felt more real estate transaction than romance. But hadn't he just arrived at her door for the sole purpose of making love to her? What was the point, other than the same pursuit that had driven him for years as he went from woman to woman, a movable feast of breasts and thighs and lips?

Was he here only for Patti's smooth skin, for the way she purred when he made love to her? Had he learned nothing in his thirty-seven years?

"Patti," he said. "I'm tired. Let's talk later."

As he drifted off, Dara whispered to him across two decades, pulling him nearer, her palms reaching around his shoulder, her grip strong. "I feel better being close," she said.

7

What's with you?" Yvette asked at the office coffee maker. Dara picked up the glass pot, its bottom sticky from years of coffee drippings. "You look like you ran into a ghost."

"Is it that obvious?" Dara poured burnt coffee into Yvette's mug.

"New chapter in the annals of Matthew-is-a-first-class-dick?"

Dara shook her head. "For once, no... The mother of an old ex died." She felt Adam's presence at her side during Pearl and Pearl's Caldwell performances in the cherry-paneled Caldwell Hall, the sound of two pianos reverberating as though streamed through a hall of mirrors.

"Sounds like nothing, right?" Dara said.

Yvette took a sip of coffee. "This is motor oil. Time for a latte?"

Dara glanced at her watch. "I don't teach until one thirty. I was going to try to work."

"Skip it, you won't get anything done in this state."

"Why do I care?" Dara said, as they settled into a corner at Center City Java.

"The old ones are the heartaches," Yvette said. "Was he your first?"

Dara nodded. "He was a violinist. Is a violinist."

"Where'd you meet?"

"Through music."

Isaac had walked Dara across the Twenty-First Street Music School's all-purpose room to introduce her to Maestro Charles Jones, who was reviewing violin bowings with Adam Pearl.

"Charles, this is Dara Kingsley, the newest member of the viola section."

"Delighted, Miss Kingsley," Jones said in that deep, resonant voice she'd heard from the Academy of Music's second balcony. "You'll share a stand with Miss Walker." He aimed his baton toward the back of the violas. "Have you met Adam Pearl? He's our concertmaster and a student at the Caldwell Institute of Music. Studies with Yuri Zablonsky, the first violinist in the Caldwell String Quartet. He'll show you how we do things."

"Nice to meet you," Adam said. His hair was in a short ponytail. He had deep-brown eyes, a strong handshake, and a smile that shone like the back of a violin.

Dara wound her way through the labyrinth of music stands, chairs, and players. Her stand partner, Barbara Walker, shouted above the cacophony of players warming up. "You're inside on this stand, so you turn pages. Play the bottom line in any section where two different parts are marked. How long have you been studying with Mr. Koroff?"

"I started in September. You?"

"I'm a sophomore in the conservatory here. He's supposed to have students in every major orchestra. I hope so, because I need a job when I get out of here. Shhh." Adam Pearl tapped his music stand with his bow. "He's cute, don't you think?"

Everyone fell silent. Adam motioned the principal oboe for an A to tune the brass. An upsurge of sound came from the back of the room. "Woodwinds," Adam said, looking supremely confident even though he was only a year or two older than Dara. "Strings," Adam said, sitting down to the third oboe A. Dara adjusted her pegs and rested her viola upright in her lap.

Charles Jones stepped up to a black music stand, flattened to hold his score. "*Finlandia*. Brass, we are in a small space. Save your chops for the end of the piece." He lifted his baton, scanned the orchestra to make sure all eyes were on him, and placed the downbeat.

Enveloped in a blast of brass, Dara could hardly count the rests. The percussion entered, more brass, then a woodwind choir, and finally the strings. After a minute, Charles Jones tapped his music stand to signal the orchestra to stop. Dara was the last to put down her instrument. Barbara leaned over. "Watch him or he'll yell at you."

"The balance is off." Jones flipped his score back to the beginning "Less trombone and more French horn." He raised his hands, then set down his baton as another point occurred to him. "Timpani," Jones said, eying the percussion section. "Your entrance is important; your sound cuts through the orchestra. Attack it exactly, or we'll lose the rhythmic drive."

Again he lifted his baton, and again an explosion of brass. Again he put down his baton. "Think arctic cold, Finland, tundra. Pure, icy sound. I need to hear both sections of violins on your runs; you're not together." He raised his baton. When Dara lifted her viola, Barbara poked her. "He said violins only." Dara winced.

Maestro Jones rehearsed the first and second violins separately, then together. He shook his head. "Mr. Pearl, give them some fingerings." Adam rose and played several of the runs in rapid succession, leaning forward to show the violins his left hand. He had excellent hand position. The violin section shuffled their feet in approval as he sat down.

Jones raised his baton once more. "Letter G, all eyes on me," the maestro said, glaring at the last stand of violas. "No talking during rehearsal." Dara was mortified.

Barbara continued dispensing wisdom at the break. "It's going to be an all-Sibelius program; Symphony No. 2 for the second half. Jones has a thing for Sibelius. They say he'd be a world-famous conductor if it weren't for his name. You can't have an international career if you're named Charles Jones." Dara stared wide-eyed. She was in awe of Charles Jones, name or no name.

"Our spring concert is at the Academy of Music," Barbara said.

"Wow!" Dara hurried over to her case to put more rosin on her bow.

She felt a hand tap her shoulder. "Do you like the orches-tra?" Adam asked. He stood close.

"I love it! Is it true we're playing at the Academy of Music?" She could feel herself blushing.

"We always play our final concert there. The acoustics are out of this world. Have you been backstage?"

She laughed. "No."

The maestro tapped his baton on his black stand to reassemble the group. Barbara was right; Adam was quite something.

"His parents are famous pianists. His mother was, I mean," Dara said to Yvette, stirring her latte. "She wasn't thrilled about me."

Yvette smiled. "I would have thought you were the type every mother takes to."

"Other than my own? I was at such a disadvantage," Dara said. "The Pearls would invite me to dinner and the three of them would go on about repertoire and musicians—people who were names from the radio to me. It was as ordinary for them as talking about brands of toothpaste. I was completely intimidated." Dara brushed her braid behind her. "I was god-damn sixteen. Weren't we supposed to be hanging around our lockers instead of playing in the Academy of Music?"

"Not me," Yvette said. "Look, my father is Jamaican and my mother is Guadeloupean. They may love that I'm a professor of Caribbean literature at a fancy university, but they do not, I repeat do not, love that I love women. That was not cool in the West Philly of my youth, and it isn't a whole lot better now. It's true that I spent a lot of eleventh grade scheming how to get Loretta over for a sleepover. But my parents didn't have a clue. I was obsessed with her. She was boy crazy; everyone was, except me. You've only known me with Carmen. Thank sweet Jesus she came into my life and decided to stay. I went through some crazy shit before her."

Dara sighed. "I'm sorry."

"For what?"

"For how bloody hard everything is. Even when it's not hard. Like this," Dara said, gesturing round her. "Coffee, friends, an academic career. What do I have to complain about?"

"The human condition?"

Dara laughed. "That's why we study literature. What is it about 'youth'? It's molten lava. The intensity. The emotions. You spend the rest of your life having them erupt at inopportune times."

"Profound, Professor Kingsley."

"Enough for an espresso brownie?"

"Sure."

"His name was Adam," Dara said, handing Yvette half a brownie on a napkin. "He was nothing like his parents. He was gentle and welcoming. I was a goner by the time I played my first concert at the Academy of Music. He gave me an insider's tour. I was dumbstruck."

Dara had arrived early to the Academy of Music, dressed in a long black skirt and black leotard, hugging her viola case and tiptoeing quietly through to stage left. The stage was empty, with an array of chairs and music stands, the percussion section set up—the timpani's copper bowls gleaming under stage lights—and a few double basses lying on their sides beside the players' stools.

Players milled around backstage, chatting and warming up. Dara went to unpack her case and bumped into Adam Pearl talking with Maestro Jones. The maestro, elegant in black tails, his silver hair combed down to just below his collar, shook her hand. "Delighted you've joined the orchestra, Miss Kingsley. I'd better be off," he said. "I need to get reacquainted with my scores before my first downbeat."

"He's way too modest. He had those scores memorized three months ago," Adam said, as if Dara were intimately familiar with the profession. As if it were part of Adam's regular routine to talk to her. As if they knew each other.

"Want to look around?" Adam asked. With his dark hair

falling to his collar, he looked older—and, if possible, more gorgeous—in a tuxedo. He led her through the wings, pointing out the elaborate lighting system and apparatus for changing scenery during ballet or opera performances.

"How do you know your way around so well?" Dara asked.

"My parents." His answer seemed to close the subject. She followed him down the hidden stairwell under the stage to the dark hollow that gave the hall its celebrated acoustics. "Here's the reason you can hear the clarinet warming up in the midst of all the other players even if you're in the second balcony," Adam said in a whisper, his voice echoing. She trembled at his proximity. "We need to head back," he said, a hand at the small of her back, his touch like lightning.

Upstairs, students had begun straggling onstage. Dara heard scales and arpeggios, and a few strains of concertos from the advanced violin students. The French horns were playing snippets of *Finlandia*. There was so much room onstage between the stands that for the first time, Dara didn't have to worry about backing her chair into the trombones or poking Barbara with her bow.

The lights dimmed and the thick cream-colored door at stage right opened for Adam. Walking down an aisle between the first and second violins, he took his place at the concertmaster's desk. He looked in command, lifting his bow to signal the oboe A.

The door opened again, for Maestro Jones—baton in his right hand, his left smoothing his silver hair. He faced the orchestra and motioned them to rise, then turned and bowed to the applause. Turning back around, he brought his hands down for the players to be seated.

A mammoth brass choir filled the hall. Dara held her instrument against the swath of skin exposed by the scoop of her leotard, her viola in full embrace. She inclined her head left to hear herself better within the complex sounds of the orchestra. The pleasure of playing in this hall, with Adam, washed over her.

"Adam wasn't the problem," Dara said to Yvette, coming out of her reverie. "And his father wasn't either. He was a nice man. It was his mother, who just died. She terrified me. She didn't think I was serious enough about music."

"Stage mother, eh?" Yvette said.

"No, stage mothers are posers. These people—the Pearls—were not posers. Mrs. Pearl played like a goddess. The first time I heard his parents play, I was at a summer music thing."

"What's a 'summer music thing'?"

"A school where the Caldwell and Juilliard faculty came to teach. We lived on a Temple University campus outside Philly—a place called Briarly, in Bucks County. Plexiglas-soundproofed practice rooms; two separate orchestras; chamber music coaching. I was in heaven."

"So, not your typical summer camp? Some of us spent summers scooping ice cream at Baskin-Robbins in the swamp that is Philadelphia in July."

"Fair enough."

"Beats melting ice cream, I guess."

Dara laughed. "I was lucky as sin to go. My teacher, Isaac Koroff, was in residence. Adam was there too. It was my first summer away from home. I went to a concert that blew my mind. I went to a lot of concerts, actually, but there was this one. The program was the same piece played twice—first, the Brahms Piano Quintet in F Minor for two violins, viola, cello, and piano. Brahms wrote an earlier version for two pianos. Adam and his quintet played the first half, and his parents played the two-piano version for the second half."

"All in the family. White people's version of the Jackson Five."

"Ha, ha. It was a small concert, no more than seventy-five people seated in a semicircle in a large classroom. That concert was when I crossed from puppy love over to real love," Dara said.

"What the hell does that mean?"

"I have no idea, just that it was important. There were five students, four of them girls—a violinist, violist, cellist, and pianist. Adam wore a white oxford shirt—collar open—and black pants."

"Sexy, eh?"

"Well, yes." Even in the fluorescent lights, Adam's dark hair shone. Dara recalled the way he put his ear to his instrument to check his tuning, then rested his violin upright on his lap. "I was so smitten," Dara said, "it hurt."

Directly in Dara's line of vision, Adam gave the signal, knees spread, bow poised in midair.

The quintet began in unison before the piano broke out and goaded the four strings forward. On top of the pulsating keyboard, the violist entered, her sound thick and dark. The second movement was soulful. Again the viola spoke, undergirding Adam's sweet line. The way he enveloped his violin, the way he leaned into his instrument! The other players watched him for rhythmic guidance. He made no extraneous movement, signaling their entrances with a flick of hair or a quickened breath.

What kind of a boyfriend would Adam be? Dara felt winded imagining his touch. His right arm technique was glorious; it was impossible to hear his bow changes. She was entranced by his embrace of the instrument, his crinkled brow.

In the middle of the third movement, a fugue broke out. Adam moved to the edge of his chair, as if poised to leap. The performers harnessed the music's passion and energy.

And then they stopped—an abrupt ending, followed by silence.

A haunting introduction to the fourth movement came next. The strings pushed toward harmonic dissonance. Just in time, the movement transformed to a romp, before driving to the end.

Dara was suspended in a stratosphere where music reigned supreme and love was possible. She ached to remain there. But audience members were getting up. The chairs were being rear-ranged. Dara slipped into the summer evening, trying to collect herself. If only she lived in a world surrounded by such music, if only she could learn to play like that, if only Adam loved her.

"Let's be clear," Yvette said with authority, stirring her coffee. "This is not about the mother. It's about the son."

"I never think about him." Dara knew she sounded absurd.

"I change my hair color when I'm feeling this tortured," Yvette said. Yvette's latest style was closely shaven, the left side of her head dyed pink.

"I wish I had the nerve," Dara said. "I haven't even had a trim in three years."

"I finally managed to kiss Loretta—once, in the spring of eleventh grade," Yvette said. "We were outside a school dance. It was late and we were stoned. She was into it, passionate—and ashamed. I hated her shame but there was nothing I could do. She moved away at the end of the year. I never saw her again."

"That's so sad," Dara said. Yvette was grounded, dwelling in the moment. "But I take some comfort that you could fixate on a crush too."

"It's true she broke my heart," Yvette said, "but fortunately, we grow up."

"I'm trying my best," Dara said.

Dara returned to the Briarly classroom at the end of inter-mission. Everything was changed; there were now two pianos, facing each other like matched puzzle pieces. Adam, holding his violin case, appeared in the chair next to hers.

"I'll be able to see my father's hands on the keyboard from here, but not my mother's," he said, as if he and Dara had left off midconversation. "It's always either one piano or the other."

"Adam." Dara's cheeks were hot. "You were fantastic."

He smiled. "Thanks. Great piece, isn't it?"

The audience broke into applause for the entrance of Victor and Adele Pearl. Towering over his petite wife, Victor placed his left hand on his piano and his right around Adele's shoulders. They bowed, slowly and deeply, before moving to their respective instruments.

Breathing together, they began, the sound of their instruments overwhelming the small space. Two pianos facing off like that, two musicians completely in harmony with each other—a wholly unimagined concoction. And they were married!

Adele was playing first piano. She led the duo and set the tempos, conducting the ritards with a turn of her head or a raised eyebrow. Her breaths mirrored her phrasing. Unlike other two-piano teams, the Pearls alternated playing first piano—a sign of their confidence in each other, Dara thought. And what of their romance? Their passion? They slept in the same bed. They made love; they had made Adam.

At the end of the first movement, Victor raked his fingers through his curly hair, rubbed a linen handkerchief across the keys, and adjusted the height of his piano bench. He smiled at Adele and they began anew. A remarkable range emanated from each instrument, as if the two alone formed an orchestra.

Next to Dara, Adam was lost in the music. His eyes were closed, shoulders rising occasionally. His left hand steadied his violin case between his chair and Dara's, his fingers long and calloused, grace on the fingerboard, a hair's breadth from her right thigh.

Between the second and third movements, Adam stirred. "Not bad, eh?" he whispered, his lips near her ear.

Pearl and Pearl—jockeys jumping their horses over the same fence. Dara surrendered to the rest of the piece, the third and fourth movements so different from the quintet she'd just heard. After his parents galloped to the finale, Adam excused himself through the applause and hurried to greet them.

8

Seated at his mother's desk, Adam was struck by the volume and breadth of correspondence. He riffled through letters from around the world sent by students, colleagues, and former neighbors. No wonder his father hadn't known where to begin.

Dear Mr. Pearl,
Studying with Mrs. Pearl was the high point of my life. I cherish her kindness and wisdom. She was amazing while my father was dying, no demands, always a willing ear.

Adam looked up at the wall in front of him, hung with autographed portraits of famous musicians, signed with glowing tributes to Adele.

Dear Victor and Adam,
I regret that I never expressed to your beloved wife and mother how much she influenced me. She had the magic touch. She was always available to answer questions and offer suggestions without being overbearing. We'll miss her terribly.

"Beloved." Adam put down his pen. That one was from Ingrid Nordstrom, a warm and lanky blond who'd accompanied Adam in a recital fifteen years before. Ingrid had managed, with her open smile and lack of cattiness, to avoid the backstabbing, competitive stranglehold of piano class at Caldwell.

Adam had felt diminished, as if he'd missed something, when she announced her engagement to a French horn player in the Philadelphia Orchestra. By now they had a couple of kids.

Victor tapped on the door to Adele's study. "Thanks for sorting through the mounds, Adam. I'll take a nap if you don't mind."

Adam watched his father go, his back curved, shoulders slumped, his grief an extra limb. Victor had expended his energy on the vain hope that his wife could be saved. He hadn't complained and he hadn't flagged—whether he was changing Adele's bedding or playing Brahms intermezzos as she rested in the living room. He'd inhabited his caretaker role as if it had been assigned him at birth.

It hadn't always been like that.

Victor rang Adam's doorbell unexpectedly at three one afternoon.

"Dad! What's going on?" Adam's violin and bow dangled from his left hand.

"Son." Without crossing the threshold, Victor said, "Your mother has ovarian cancer…very advanced."

"What?" Adam held the door open for his father, trying to emerge from the mist of his practicing. "Dad, come in. Sit down."

Neither of them moved.

"Terminal, the doctor says."

The news left Adam gasping. His mother was indomitable, indefatigable, and above all, predictable. She had not been sick in his memory and had never been late to a lesson or a rehearsal. She had risen at the same time every morning and eaten the same breakfast (cornflakes with milk) unless she was on the road. She'd scrupulously avoided simple pleasures such as a cookie in the afternoon or a midmorning pastry.

"I think she's known about it for some time," Victor said, his face sagging in despair.

Adele's routine was unwavering, her energy legendary. She must be very, very sick to have visited a doctor.

Terminal. The word was too big for Adam to absorb.

"She never gave the slightest hint," Victor said. "Other than mentioning something about our Mozart concert and not wanting to ruin it. Can you think of anything more absurd?"

"I'll come home with you," Adam said. "Let me put my

violin away." The framework of his family was collapsing, a structure he'd taken for granted.

"How could she have kept this from me?" Victor asked. "She can be a stranger sometimes."

Adam looked up from sliding his violin into its blue satin cover. *A stranger?* Victor spent more time with Adele than with anyone else, more time than he spent with himself.

When they got to his parents', Adele was at her keyboard.

"Mother!" Adam blurted out, interrupting his mother's practicing for the first time in recent memory.

"Hello, dear," Adele said, coming up out of her practice trance. "Your father and I are playing Köchel three-sixty-five in less than two weeks. I have work to do." Who was she fooling? "What will be will be," Adele added, glancing over her shoulder at Adam before resuming her practice.

Adam felt a streak of rage, which melted to compassion. For her, for her rigidity. Adele ran on raw talent and drive, but also on unwavering conviction. She would brook neither nuance nor doubt. Ambiguity caused her stress. Adam was anguished for the suffering that would come and for the exactitude of her playing, which would let her down as surely as a double bar concluded a concerto.

Adam sat in his father's green easy chair and listened to Mozart emanate from Adele's strong, pliant fingers. He was crushed that she hadn't told him herself of her diagnosis. He felt pushed away, treated as one of the crowd.

How much worse it must be for Victor.

It occurred to Adam that Adele had a private life that she kept from Victor. Adam was surprised he hadn't considered this before. He felt naïve. What really went on inside his mother's head? If he could have comforted her, he would have. But where was the comfort with death on a fast track? More than anything, Adam wanted to lie underneath his mother's soundboard, close his eyes, and let her music wash over him.

At Adele's desk, Adam picked up Ingrid's note. If only he could eliminate a fraction of his father's pain. At the least, he could help with the condolence notes.

Ingrid had introduced him to Annette Farley. Annette played second flute in the Philadelphia Orchestra. Her playing was full of pyrotechnics, her sound lush and syrupy. Adele adored her. "Such a fine musician, such a delightful person!"

Adam and Annette had lived together for two years. He left when it dawned on him that waking up next to her made him feel desolate.

Adam tapped his pen on his mother's blotter. You either were a good musician or you weren't. That was her narrow view, a single inflexible yardstick by which to measure humanity. He felt a flicker of pity for Adele, for what she had missed.

Two weeks after learning his mother's news, Adam sat in the audience to hear his parents play Mozart with the Philadelphia Chamber Symphony. He considered the concerto's exquisitely orchestrated first movement, calling for duo-pianists playing with the precision of sewing machines. Lesser players limited their performance to the concerto's solemn side, squandering the music's beauty. The Pearls delivered both vigor and levity.

How could Adele perform as if she didn't have a care in the world?

Adam imagined his mother at her piano bench, her left elbow resting on the closed keyboard, her right arm beckoning him to sit with her. "You're all I ever wanted," she could say. "You're the best son a mother could hope for. This must be so hard for you."

Adam was being infantile; nothing like this would happen. Adele should save her courage and determination for herself. She should marshal her resources.

Adam turned around and scanned the audience. They were rapt, smiling and sated, with no idea what they were witnessing. Adam wanted to preserve his mother the way they saw her, unflappable and confident. He wanted Adele to remain tough.

He'd spent his life bristling at her authoritativeness, her drive, her slavish devotion to music, but now he craved that dependability.

The Pearls had never played so lovingly. Adele, sparkling and alert; Victor—leaning into the music toward his wife—rooted and balanced. Adam was hoarding memories: his parents' expressions; his mother's head poised to capture the shades of the orchestra; her feet on the pedals, shaping musical phrases like a sculptor polishing marble.

Adam composed a mental list of compliments to give his mother after the concert. He knew she would need them. She was in the habit of seeking Adam's advice on two-piano pieces to add to scheduled orchestra programs—whether an audience in Kansas City would be satisfied with the same musical composition as one in Phoenix—and his opinions regarding upcoming guest conductors at the Concertgebouw or the L.A. Philharmonic. Increasingly Adele leaned on Adam for guidance and reassurance. Her son was more counselor than counseled.

The family mandate was that Adam be self-reliant. Adulthood was prized, and so Adam had entered it early. (Had he, though?) Before Adele's diagnosis, the death of either parent was a remote possibility in some hazy future. Adam couldn't imagine his parents separated by anything, let alone death.

He understood nothing of what his mother was going through. He would have to carry his fear and worry alone. He had no one to confide in. Time would not stop, even for Adele.

What about Victor? Adam needed to be there for him, whatever that meant. Adele might be pretending things hadn't changed, but Victor was devastated. How would he bear the unbearable?

Adam's parents were not only the team that had raised him; they were also a public team, *the* Pearl and Pearl duo. The three Pearls were a public family, seen as talented, taut, and cohesive, where the exceptional was ordinary, and the ordinary did not exist. Adam was supposed to uphold their sterling reputation, a task that was never explicit but that had been clear since he could remember. A rupture in their threesome was unimaginable.

Adam was tired of upholding the family image.

He couldn't see where Patti fit in either.

In the Green Room after the concert, Victor, afraid his mood would shatter the veneer of normality, excused himself and slipped out.

Adam watched his mother smiling and shaking hands, going through the motions of post-concert glow. She was surrounded by a crowd of well-wishers yet looked starkly alone, as if, instead of multitudes, she'd just played to an empty hall.

Adam was gutted by her isolation.

Adam reorganized the piles on Adele's desk to clear some space, stacking letters he'd answered to one side, the remaining letters on the other. As he stood to go, he saw an envelope in the corner of his mother's blotter. Return address: Phillip Hissle. He sat down again.

The postmark was over forty years old. Adam was afraid the paper would crack as he unfolded it.

To Adele—
You won't.
You don't.
You can't.
I will.
Always.
Yours, Phillip

His mother had written something in pencil. Her notes were barely legible, faded with age.

You won't. Love me.
You don't. Love me.
You can't. Love me.
I will. Love you.
Always.

How often over the past decades had Adele opened and closed this envelope? Adam's hands shook. He was afraid he would rip the delicate paper as he reinserted the letter.

It was a mercy that Victor had asked Adam for help going through Adele's desk. And a greater mercy that Victor had slept through Adam's discovery.

PART II

We live between memory and anticipation, between the past and the future... We live in time and through time.

—George Rochberg, *The Aesthetics of Survival*

9

Adam missed the moment of his mother's death. The New Philadelphia Trio had had a concert that night. Adam wanted to cancel it, but Victor encouraged him to go ahead. What were a few hours of performance, against the dozens Adam had spent next to Adele's hospital bed, or pacing the antiseptic corridors outside her room?

Adam stopped by Adele's hospital room dressed in his tuxedo, violin case in hand. "I'll be back in a couple of hours," he said, "after the concert." As he rose to leave, it occurred to him that his mother, though comatose, might be able to hear him. He knelt by her bedside.

"The program, Mother, I thought you might want to know. It's Brahms opus eight. Thaddeus does a fine job on the cello solo. We're playing Beethoven's 'Archduke' and the Schubert E Flat too." He pressed his lips to her limp hand. Against the whirring and beeping of medical equipment he said, "You can listen, we're only a few blocks away."

Relaxed and peaceful, Adam performed his part of the trio. Maybe his mother *could* hear him, the melody penetrating the hospital walls, reminding her of all that was right and good in her world. At the end of the concert Adam took his bows, thanked his colleagues, and walked through the brisk, dark night to the hospital.

One glance at his father, staring down the fluorescent corridor, told him it was over.

"Say goodbye to her, son. You'll want to say goodbye." Victor was ashen.

A nurse had unplugged the life-prolonging wires. Adele looked more like a figure carved onto a medieval tomb than Adam's mother. She was waxen and gaunt, not the vivacious, energetic woman he had known.

Adam picked up Adele's hands. They were not yet cold. "The concert went well, Mother. I hope you heard it. The cello solo was especially gorgeous in the Brahms. Full house, balance good. Piano playing up to snuff. I played it for you, Mother," he whispered. "I imagined the music bringing you comfort for the journey. The journey." He repeated the phrase to convince himself that she was gone.

Adam sat with Adele. He tried to ignore the muffled sobs of his father, the steady squeak of nurses' shoes down the corridor, and the machines humming across the hall. He wanted—needed—to understand the fact of his mother's death.

Eventually he stood and placed his mother's limp hands together. Those ten fingers—her instrument, her voice—had had their time.

Adam flicked off the light switch. In the pale shadows Adele looked serene.

"Goodnight, Mother."

10

Thaddeus Collier barreled into the Caldwell Concert Hall, cello case strapped to his back. "How're you holding up?" he said, thumping Adam on the shoulder. With his fiery beard and burly frame, Thaddeus could be manhandling a chainsaw rather than gripping a cello between his legs.

"I'm worried about my father," Adam said. And Adele and Hissle. And the possibility that Adele, whom Adam had assumed was single-minded, was becoming more complex. Adam was awakening to a sense of missed opportunity, to a dearth that was not quite grief. He'd had a preconceived notion of grief, and it was not this.

He'd underestimated his mother, failed to get to know her. He was old enough to have tried and was paying for his lack of effort. "Death is so final," he said. Thaddeus looked as if Adam were speaking in tongues. "I know it's obvious," Adam added, "but it's true. Do you think a child can ever know their parent?"

"Don't go all moonbeamy on me," Thaddeus said, with a laugh that rumbled like thunder. "And try not to worry, your father will be okay. Give him time. Ever hear the story of when Peter Schidlof died? The violist in the Amadeus Quartet? The Amadeus announced his death and dissolved themselves at the same time. Sort of sweet, huh? Like a marriage, acknowledging that Schidlof was irreplaceable. Makes me think of your mom."

"Nice." Adam was afraid he might cry. He pictured his parents across the living room from each other, his mother having set the schedule for the day. "Victor, your attack isn't clear," she would shout over the music. "More left hand!" And Victor would reply, "Adele, shouldn't we try that movement a hair slower?" or "Let's warm up the staccato notes in measures one twenty-four to one thirty; they sound like machine-gun fire."

Their trust in each other was ironclad. But had Adele been deserving of Victor's trust?

"Regards from Natalia," Thaddeus said, taking off his coat.

Adam colored. "She's in town?"

"No. Talked to her last night."

Adam walked up the three steps to the stage and found two music stands from the back for Thaddeus and himself. He raised the piano lid partway, feeling a longing for Natalia's full hips, her legs tangoing with her cello. The first night he'd gone to Natalia's, she greeted him in a brightly colored caftan. When she bent over to restrain her golden retriever, her bare breasts swung inside her robe. She stood up and pressed herself against him, her palm pushing toward his groin. Adam was so besotted, he routinely missed cues during rehearsal. "You're playing first violin," Natalia would say in her throaty Russian voice. "You should be riding us!"

"No surprise, Natalia's burning up the Windy City," Thaddeus said, grabbing his sheet music and joining Adam onstage. "She has a guy in the bass section and a rich lawyer on the side, married of course. If I know Natalia, there have to be more."

Adam picked up two chairs from the wings to put in front of the music stands. He was peevish over Natalia's men and envious that Thaddeus was in touch with her. He sat down and tightened his bow, feeling cheap—and shallow—for falling for Natalia in the first place. He'd known their relationship wouldn't amount to anything.

"Your mother was one in a million," Thaddeus said, taking his chair. "She could criticize without crushing egos. That's a talent! She coached my first-year chamber group. We were studying the Mozart G Minor Piano Quartet. The pianist was aggressive and whiny; I still can't figure out how he managed to be both. I was ready to kill him. We're all screaming at each other when your mother walks in. Without missing a beat, she says, 'Close your eyes!' She has us each play the first two lines of the slow movement, separately. When we finish, it's silent as a tomb. She whispers, 'That's what we want to hear. Those four parts. This isn't a competition; no one needs to outplay anybody. We want a palette of colors. If one of them is missing, the painting is not only incomplete, it's vandalized.'

"I felt like some wacko slashing a da Vinci canvas," Thaddeus said. "I calmed down and focused on the music instead of decking the pianist. It was genius on your mother's part."

Adam smiled. "Funny," he said, holding his violin to his ear and plucking the strings to check the tuning. "She was competitive as hell but bowed before the composer. 'Composer is king,' she used to say."

"All I saw was charm," Thaddeus said.

The concert hall door opened, and Patti walked up the aisle. "Welcome to the New Philadelphia Trio," Adam said. "In case you don't know us, we're a frequent feature on the Philadelphia music scene and up and down both coasts," he added jokingly. With Vladimir Rofsky's splendid piano playing, they landed regular recording contracts too. Patti would be a good substitute, but Adam hoped Vladimir made a quick recovery.

Thaddeus's mane of red hair shook as he pumped Patti's hand. "Thanks for pinch-hitting." Turning to Adam, he continued. "Nice tribute to Adele, having one of her students play with us."

Adam nodded. He wished Thaddeus would stop talking about Adele. He'd spent his life asking for something that his mother had denied him but apparently had given freely to everyone else. How many times had she come up after one of Adam's performances and said, "Your trio should consider another agent. You could be getting overseas bookings." Before he'd even packed up his instrument! Why couldn't she appreciate the music he made in his trio? He didn't want to travel the world like his parents. Home was a place where you lived, not a place you returned to after spending two-thirds of the year on the road. Still, Adam wondered what he'd done to make a home. And why this was all he could think about right now.

Patti sat down, arranged her music, and tested the keyboard—chords roiling—filling the hall with piano sound.

Nobody would know Patti and I sleep together, Adam thought, wondering if his relationship with her was an improvement over what he'd had with Natalia. He was going to disappoint Patti and was a fraud for not speaking up. He didn't want to be closer to her. He didn't want to have the conversation she wanted. He didn't want to live with her, not because of her, he realized, but because of him. He couldn't remember a time when he'd craved solitude more. If only he could stop time, hole up in his apartment, and stare out his picture windows.

"Shall we start with the Mendelssohn?" Adam asked, trying to shake off his gloom.

Patti played A for tuning, then added the expected F and D in thirds below.

Adam picked up his violin and cued the opening. Thaddeus dug in, swaying to the beat. Patti embraced the keyboard, flicking pages as they sprinted by.

They stopped for Adam and Thaddeus to discuss bowings. "Let's try it from measure sixty-five," Adam said. "It's Patti and me playing alone there."

Someone opened the door and crept into the back of the hall. Thaddeus leaned toward Adam. "Isn't that Phillip Hissle?"

From the corner of his eye, Adam watched Hissle, dressed in a gray winter coat, settle into a seat. Adam missed his cue.

He sat up straighter, as if ramrod posture might tamp his anger.

During their break, Adam wandered to the back of the hall. "How's your ankle, Phillip?"

"Your father wouldn't let your mother accompany me in a recital," Hissle said.

It took Adam a moment. "What recital?"

"It never happened." Hissle put on his fedora and hobbled out.

Adam's resolve gave way to empty bravado. He walked back to pick up his violin, pressing his left thumb into his index finger—first finger for violinists, second for pianists. It was a nervous habit, pressing those two fingers together, as if they channeled feelings oblivious to the rest of him. A callus ridged the tip of his index finger from his violin strings. The lowest string, G, required more pressure to get a clean, focused sound; the highest, E, was thinner, cutting a sharper line across his fingertips. Calluses were string players' livelihoods—critical for endurance and precision, the means to make intricate adjustments to intonation and tone.

What was Hissle talking about? There was nothing Victor wouldn't let Adele do.

The trio picked up where they'd left off—Patti blanketing the keyboard and Thaddeus wrapped around his instrument, fixed on the pulse. Notes flew by. Adam watched the music with little thought to his playing. What had his mother been hiding?

Thaddeus waved his bow. "We're not together."

"Patti, you're pushing the tempo," Adam said, trying to keep the edge out of his voice. "Please don't rush us."

Patti nodded and ran her index finger across her bottom lip. Adam had seen that motion. Patti across his bed. Oh lord. Patti.

"Adam, you're distracted," Thaddeus said.

Life had been simpler before Adam opened Hissle's envelope.

"It's good of you to rehearse so soon after your loss," Thaddeus continued. "But we need dynamic contrast in this movement." He smiled. "Gotta give the audience what they paid for."

Adam straightened up. "Let's go back to measure ninety-two." He raised his violin and motioned to start.

Patti arched over the keyboard. Adam wondered if she was wearing a slip.

For years, Adam hadn't given Hissle a thought. Not since Dara, and not much then. Hissle had been her chamber music coach and, later, teacher. More recently, Hissle was just another Caldwell faculty member whose students weren't particularly notable.

Patti's descending chords reversed and started climbing.

Finally, she'd taken charge of the tempo. She was an excellent pianist, even with her tendency to rush.

They finished discussing changes to the Mendelssohn and moved onto Dvořák. Adam wondered whether his father suspected anything about Hissle but had no idea how to ask. It would be too cruel; Hissle's letter would violate Victor's grief. Adam leaned into his violin and crescendoed to the next *forte*.

11

Victor sat in his green easy chair, absentmindedly studying his hands. He should be practicing. His left index finger was getting dangerously stiff, and the knuckle on his right thumb was beginning to bother him. It was madness to let his hands atrophy.

On the other hand, why bother? His performance calendar was canceled. He had nothing to look forward to. His piano was starting to collect dust, which hadn't occurred in living memory. Weeks and months could go by, time accumulating like geologic sediment, layers of grief's striations.

He paged through Adele's scrapbooks, her idle-hands-are-the-devil's-workshop activity. She never did understand the concept of rest. The entries pierced like shards of glass.

Pearl and Pearl Perform at the Metropolitan Museum of Art

New York, November 7, 1966. Young duo-pianists Victor and Adele Pearl opened last night's program with Brahms's 21 Hungarian Dances for four hands. A brilliant selection for displaying the Pearls' expansive expressive range, the piece also showcased the two-pianists' impressive technical virtuosity…

Victor recalled embracing his wife in the Green Room that night. Patting her belly, he'd asked, "How did the baby like the music?"

"Not too much kicking."

The light from the wall sconces across the room twinkled in her eyes. "Adele, you were wonderful."

"We let the tempo get away from us at the end," Adele said matter-of-factly. "We'll be faulted for our dynamics. They'll say we were too excitable."

"I don't think we should be too concerned," Victor said, stroking the pathway down her backbone.

She touched his forearm. "We should say hello to the people coming in."

Following her toward a group of well-wishers, Victor saw the door swing open. "My God, that's my mother!"

Victor hadn't seen his mother for two years. She wouldn't answer his periodic notes. He had dreamed of this moment, when he would stand in reflected glory as he introduced her to Adele. He elbowed his way over to his mother, his height accentuated by his tailcoat, and looked above the crowd to see the elder Mrs. Pearl presenting a cloud of peach roses to Adele.

"How wonderful of you to come," Adele was saying.

"Mother, may I introduce you to Adele Hammond Pearl?"

"Too late," his mother said.

Adele beamed.

"You didn't tell me she was pregnant," the elder Mrs. Pearl said. "You two...you two sounded..." She dabbed her eyes with a tissue. "Will you stay with me the next time you come to New York?"

"Of course!" Adele said cheerfully.

"Go greet your adoring fans." Victor's mother turned to leave. "And congratulations." Managing a half smile, she closed the door behind her.

Well-wishers pressed into Victor, who was in a commotion of pride and frustration. He turned to Adele. "Thank you for being so gracious. After the way she's treated you."

"Why look back?" Adele said. "There's no point in checking old sores. Life's too short. I'll never have time to learn all the music in the repertoire." Casting him a pert, sideways glance, she dove into the crowd.

BERNSTEIN CONDUCTS THE
SAN FRANCISCO SYMPHONY

San Francisco, March 7, 1976. Leonard Bernstein had the audience leaping from their seats by the end of *West Side Story.* It was thus gratifying to hear an equally sparkling rendering of Francis Poulenc's Concerto in D Minor for Two Pianos and Orchestra by formidable duo-pianists Victor and Adele Pearl, making their San Francisco debut....

Victor and Adele had just taken their last bows. They walked offstage through the wings where Herman Stickman, their agent, was waving a pink phone message. He guided them to the stage manager's office. "There's been an accident. Adam's broken something," he said, dialing a rotary phone.

"You don't know more than that?" Victor asked anxiously.

"I got you the message, didn't I?" Stickman glowered and handed the receiver to Adele.

"Let's stay calm until we know what the problem is," Adele said. She glanced at her watch, the one she wore for concerts, with the thin silver band and narrow oval face. "Oh lord, it's the middle of the night there, isn't it?... Hello, Bella, is that you? I'm sorry it's so late; it must be two in the morning there. What happened?"

Victor put his palms against the doorjamb and pushed as if he were doing a bench press.

"Which wrist?" Cupping her hand over the receiver, Adele whispered, "It's the right one. Adam fell off the jungle gym at school. But he only has to wear a cast for four weeks, so it must not be a compound fracture. My goodness, is he still awake?" Adele continued. "A lot of pain, I understand. Hello, Adam. What are you doing up this late? I'm sorry it hurts. Let me put your father on."

Handing the phone to Victor, Adele said, "Well, it doesn't sound like it will do permanent damage to his bow arm."

"Son, I wish I could be there with you," Victor said, unsettled by his son in pain. "Just a minute." He covered the receiver. "Maybe we should cancel our recital and fly out in the morning."

"Victor, it's a broken wrist," Adele said. "We'll be back Monday. Let me talk to him."

Adele took the phone again. "We love you so much; we'll be

home the day after tomorrow. Daddy and I have a major recital that we can't cancel. Bella will take care of you until we get home. She always does."

Victor shook his head. "He's nine years old," he whispered, loud enough for Adam to hear. "We're across the continent."

"I know it's not the same," Adele was saying into the phone. "But we'll be home as soon as we can. Excuse me, honey? The day after tomorrow. Now run along to bed, it's late."

"We can reschedule our recital," Victor said after Adele hung up. "Things happen."

Stickman's face creased in fury. "You're not canceling! I had to move heaven and earth to get the date and the hall. I am not refunding every bloody person who purchased tickets. We have a full house and a guaranteed review in the *Chronicle* and the *Examiner*. It's just a broken wrist."

Adele motioned to Stickman to be quiet. "Victor," she said, taking his hands in hers, "these are awful decisions. But it's only one more day. Adam will be fine. We'll be home before you know it. We're not scheduled for another tour for several months."

They were booked to stay at the Mark Hopkins that night. A gigantic urn of fresh flowers was displayed on the reception desk. Victor's patent-leather concert shoes made no sound on the plush purple carpeting.

"My heels are sinking!" Adele laughed excitedly.

Their room was filled with stately blond furniture. The bed was all in white, spread with a crisp down comforter and starched sheets. Victor took his time unfastening the hooks on his cummerbund. "Adele. Maybe we should go home a day early."

She reached up to help him unbutton his tuxedo shirt. "We'll be home the day after tomorrow."

"I didn't think of asking Stickman if anyone in town could substitute for one of us if the other went back."

"Victor!" Adele pulled back. "It's us they want to hear, not some last-minute stand-in. We're Pearl and Pearl, remember? Please, it's only a wrist."

When they lay down in the inviting expanse of their bed, Adele reached for Victor from behind, her hand traveling up from his knee. Victor turned around and kissed the top of her head. "Not tonight, dear."

Victor found no further concert programs in that album, just pictures of Adam and the family: Adam playing in the leaves in Rittenhouse Square; climbing a cherry tree by the Schuylkill River; posing with his first full-size violin next to their pianos; student recitals. Pictures Victor must have taken, though he couldn't recall doing so.

Even with these pictures, Victor was haunted by Adele's *no*'s that he'd witnessed over the years, Adele declining Adam's small requests. *No, dear, your father will take you to the doctor today; my schedule won't allow it. It's Daddy's job to get you shoes; I have to practice.* Piles of his wife's *no*'s accumulated into something too big for Victor to fix. Whenever he would express concern to Adele, she became agitated. He shuddered recalling Adam's looks of disappointment.

Victor considered the peculiarity of Adele's love, artlessly expressed or hidden from view. At least the photos in the album told a narrative of family, of Adele's engagement with their son. Maybe her mother love was quivering in another dimension like an unsent letter.

12

Dara grabbed a doughnut and orange juice and headed to her Briarly practice room. Her case was open by 7:15 a.m. She played forty-five minutes of left-hand exercises followed by forty-five minutes for her right hand. Moving her bow slowly across the strings, Dara owned her morning practice space. It was where she tried to produce warm, fat sounds. The campus slept while she crawled through Ševčík. No one would tolerate the tedium of an hour and a half of Ševčík this early.

So she was taken aback when she heard violin chords next door. Not technical etudes, but music, penetrating the wall. Maybe it was two violinists practicing a duet, the sounds were so complex. Dara sat down, set her viola upright in her lap, and closed her eyes. On the other side of the wall was enchantment, a pure, clean sound, no scratches, no bumps. Finally she could no longer contain her curiosity. She pushed open the door to her practice room and peeked through the Plexiglas door beside her.

A tall young man stood with his back to her, facing his music stand. He was engrossed in his playing, barely watching the notes go by. Adam Pearl. He was on to the second movement, a fugue with double stops—chords that produced the sound of several instruments. His rib cage expanded in time to the fugue, in and out, rhythmically aligned with the music. His extending bow arm gave the illusion that his body filled the whole practice cubicle.

Dara stood open-mouthed, clutching her braid over her left shoulder. She lost her sense of time and forgot that she could be seen listening in. He was beautiful.

At the end of the third movement, sensing someone watching, Adam turned around. It didn't occur to Dara to move; she wanted to hear more. But he had seen her and was opening his door. "What're you doing here?"

Dara was crimson. "Listening." She tugged her braid. "I mean practicing. But I had to stop when I heard you. Only I didn't know it was you; I just had to hear the music." She'd been caught. "It was great. What was it?"

Adam laughed. "Bach. Ridiculously difficult. It's early," he said. "I sometimes take the plunge when no one's around. I thought I was the only one up at this hour. It turns out," he said, "you're awake." He gazed at her. "What are you working on?"

"Ševčík."

"Oh yes, you're an Isaac Koroff student."

Dara was overcome with embarrassment. She left and returned to her practice room.

In no time the fourth movement's rapid-fire arpeggios came from Adam's practice room.

Dara couldn't continue with him playing next door. Lugging her viola case back to the girls' dormitory, she burst into her room.

"What the hell time is it?" her roommate Lily Rios asked, peering out of the covers. "Jesus, you're a maniac. Is it even light?" She sat up and cracked the window shade, squinted, and closed it immediately.

Lily was a Filipino pianist from Los Angeles. Dara was in the habit of going to Lily's practice room to pick her up for dinner, mostly to watch Lily spread-eagled on the keyboard like a beefy man about to pick up a refrigerator. Lily was a short girl, but she pounded out music, her small hands stretched like rubber bands, her piano shaking with the same power that imperiled the ribs of people she hugged.

Each evening, the pattern was the same. "Shit. It's already dinnertime?" Lily would say, surprised when Dara gingerly entered. "I only just got started! But I can't miss a meal at these prices." Gathering up her music, she said, "Pa would kill me.

They're skipping meals back home to send me here, let alone Juilliard in September. I'm supposed to get somewhere."

Lily already was somewhere. Dara couldn't understand what was left for her to do. Her mastery of the keyboard was daunting.

"What is your problem at this ungodly hour?" Lily said, squinting at Dara.

"Adam Pearl."

"Oh, baby, you've got it bad!"

"How do you like it here on the farm?" Isaac asked, taking his pipe out of his mouth.

Dara tried to push away the image of Adam Pearl discovering her listening in. "I like it," she said.

"You got all day to practice. Are you logging the hours?"

Dara nodded. "I hope you can tell." She wondered where she could practice the next morning to avoid Adam's hearing her. On the other hand, she was dying to run into him again.

"You're doing just fine," Isaac said, with a note of self-satisfaction. "Once you start college, you'll get tied up in your books. If you were smart, you would have listened to me and gone to conservatory."

Dara could have blamed her parents for insisting on college, but honestly, she hadn't wanted to go to conservatory. There were too many things to learn, too many books to read. "I'll make it work, you'll see," she said. She intended to pull it off—an academic degree and an orchestra job after graduation. Isaac placed his students in orchestras all over the country. Dara had dreamed about the Philadelphia Orchestra, but that was a very long shot.

Isaac looked dubious. "Going to all the concerts here?"

"They're amazing."

"Good, you need to hear everything. What've you got for me today?"

"Ševčík," Dara said, rosining her bow.

There was no cheating Isaac Koroff. He was going to hear all twenty-four variations for left and right hand that he'd assigned. She would not cut corners, and his attention would not wane.

"On to Marcello," Isaac said when she finished. "We're going to learn about phrasing, how the composer drives the melody from one point to the next. You can have all the technique in the world, but if you don't know how to phrase, you're a machine, not a musician."

He picked up his viola. "How beautiful can you make it?" He puffed his pipe and played through the first two measures. "We're going to the high E here," he said. "Put your hand on my forearm," he commanded, sticking his right elbow into Dara's face. "And listen!"

Dara felt Isaac's tendons tighten as he played toward the E. "It's all in the bow," Isaac said. "My index finger bears down on the frog to intensify the sound. You won't hear any scratches. Let's hear it, daaaa da duh da da *dum*," he sang in his raspy voice. "It had better be gorgeous!" Not like his voice, Dara thought, which bore a strong resemblance to a croaking toad.

Dara made a clumsy attempt to imitate him. Isaac waved his bow. "I want to hear the first two notes as lusciously as if your life depended on it. Listen!" He took a deep breath, closed his eyes as his bow engaged the string, and milked the first two notes for all they were worth.

Together, they went note by painstaking note, Isaac's sound honey coated, Dara's a poor stepcousin. Her bow strokes were foot soldiers in an epic struggle to approach Isaac's. She didn't know how she was going to reproduce his warmth. But at least she could hear it; his succulent tone resonated within her.

On the way back to her practice room, Adam intercepted her. "Want to come to the Karminsky Quartet? They're playing in the shell tonight."

"Yes! Thank you," she remembered to add. With Adam? Tonight?

Adam was there, standing outside the entrance to the concert shell. He smiled and kissed her lightly on the mouth.

"I was worried you'd come in a different entrance."

A kiss! There was no mistaking it. Stumbling for words, she sat next to him and tucked the book she was holding into her bag.

"What's that?" he said.

"*Crime and Punishment*," she said. "First time I've read Dostoyevsky."

"Light entertainment?"

She laughed. "We didn't get beyond British literature in my high school. Crazy. I have to get a head start before college. The kids who went to fancy private schools will have read the classics."

"Who knew?"

"Have you read it?" she asked. She was too nervous to wait for an answer. "It's a nail biter. This guy Raskolnikov decides to murder a pawnbroker because he thinks she doesn't deserve to live; she's just ripping off poor people who can't feed their children, and stealing from starving students like him. So, he brains her with an axe and then her sister, who never hurt a flea, unexpectedly shows up, so he splits her head open too."

"Gruesome!" Adam said.

"I'm not giving anything away; this all happens right at the beginning." Adam was looking at her and smiling. With affection, Dara thought fleetingly.

"The Russian classics," Adam said. "Angsty heroes out murdering old women."

Dara laughed.

"Seriously," he said, "I admire you. I'm even jealous." He was? "Are you the only one around here who reads?"

"Never thought about it." Dara felt as if she were running in overdrive, unable to rein in her talking. "I'm lost without a book. I can't remember a time when I couldn't read. Used to entertain myself in the car with the owner's manual. My mother says I wasn't even five."

"Smart girl," Adam said. "I wish I read more."

"You could make the time!"

He looked surprised. "Maybe you're right. You must study a lot."

"Study?" Where was he going with this? She sounded like a blabbermouth. "I guess. Isaac gives me grief for spending too much time with books, but I swear I practice hours for him." Should she have said this to Adam? "Especially here. I've never worked so hard in my life. Isaac must realize I'll have to study more at Penn. He's on my case about it. I'm starting this fall."

"University of Pennsylvania?"

"Yeah."

"You're staying in Philly for college?"

She tried to focus. "I love Isaac, so I wanted to go to college near him. And it's cool to study with him here. I love the concerts." And you sitting next to me, she wanted to add. "I save all the programs." At concerts she was getting better at hearing distinct harmonies and separate instrumental lines threading together to make a musical whole. She was developing viola ears—an ability to hear inside voices, to follow the music from the harmonies instead of the melodies. She thought that players in sync were engaged in a higher form of communication than that allowed by words. She was excited about the intensity of her musical work, and that it was paying off.

Most students stayed in their rooms at night and got high, including, occasionally, Lily, though she was usually in her practice room until two or three in the morning. "I come to the shell every night," Dara said.

"I've seen you," Adam said.

"You have?" Where had he been sitting? She felt a pang for those missed evenings.

"You're always reading," Adam said, as if he were answering her. "I like the Karminsky Quartet. But not so much Phillip Hissle. He's kind of coarse."

"Isaac is having me take his chamber music class in the fall."

She wanted to keep talking, but the audience started clapping. The four men in the Karminsky Quartet took their places onstage, tuned, and began to play Haydn's "Emperor" Quartet. The musicians looked far away, dwarfed by the big stage and expansive bleachers. Mr. Hissle sat on the outside next to the cellist, their bows moving up and down in parallel, as neat and orderly as the music.

With Adam next to her, Dara had trouble listening. What had he said about Hissle? *Coarse*—that was it. When the music got loud, Hissle's silver hair fell into his eyes. Adam was right, Hissle could sound scratchy. A contrast to Isaac's mellow, rich sound.

The lights came on for intermission. Adam leaned nearer and asked, "What did you think?"

She'd been thinking about Adam and not much else. "They're good," she said.

"It's not a life," Adam said. "They're on the road all the time, living out of suitcases. Even my parents don't travel that much."

Dara reminded herself that his parents were Pearl and Pearl. "What's it like for you?"

"Nice that you asked," Adam said. Gently he brushed the back of his fingers down her cheek. She was burning. "Everyone assumes it's great," he said quietly. "You're the first person who's ever asked me, who's ever questioned the whole setup."

"Does it bother you?" She didn't know if she was asking about her question or his home life.

"My parents are away a lot," he said. "I'm living at home even though I'm at Caldwell as a college student. It's like a private apartment; the place feels empty... We don't have a regular family." He inched closer. "May I?" he asked, before putting his arm around her.

She leaned into his chest, the first time she had ever been this close to a boy.

He rubbed her shoulder and brought her nearer. "We don't sit around and watch TV after dinner, or whatever it is other families do. I can't imagine what that must be like," he said.

The lights went down. Dara wondered if her thumping heart was audible. Having pianists for parents seemed so inviting. Listening to all those gorgeous pieces. The Pearls must know everything about music, Dara mused, unlike her own parents. On the other hand, she remembered her mother saying that you couldn't tell anything about a family from the outside. The ones who present perfect facades are often the most messed up. Still, if you had parents like Adam's, you could go to free concerts whenever you wanted.

The Karminsky launched into Bartók's sixth quartet. Dara was assaulted by its dissonance. She peeked sideways at Adam. He was enraptured; he understood what he was listening to. She tried to pay attention to Bartók, but there was only Adam, next to her. He had kissed her and wrapped his arm around her.

They walked toward the dorms. "Do you need to go in now?" Adam asked.

"No."

"Take a walk?" He put his arm around her again. Slowly, hesitantly, she put hers around him. She wanted to slide her hand up and down his ribs but felt too scared. They walked toward a bench outside the darkened dining hall.

"Adam?"

"Yes?" His voice was intimate, private.

She had questions, a thousand wonderments about how she had gotten here, with him, tonight. He was the best-looking boy she'd ever seen. He played his violin as if in a tender embrace, where she was now.

"How did you come to study violin?" she asked.

He laughed. "Is that what you want to know? No one really remembers. The story goes that Yuri Zablonsky was over for dinner and asked if he could get his hands on me. I was four. I guess the rest is history."

"Do your parents mind that you don't play piano?"

"I do, passably enough. Supposedly I was picking out tunes

in diapers. But I don't have time now. Yuri put his foot down. My parents decided I would benefit from having my own identity. Surprising, if you knew them."

"What do you mean?"

"They're pretty tunnel vision, especially my mother."

"Ah." She didn't know how to ask more. It occurred to her that she might have the kind of family Adam wanted—although her older brother was annoying, and her parents were constantly telling her she should study more and practice less. "What's it like at Caldwell?" Dara said.

"You ask a lot of questions! What about you?"

"I asked you first," she said, grinning.

"After two years, you get the hang of it. Practice and rehearse and practice some more. No time to learn everything you need to. I only have two more years."

"Do you have anything more to learn?"

He looked at her, startled. "You're serious, aren't you? You couldn't ask that question if you come from where I do." He slid his fingers under her braid, down the smooth skin at the back of her neck. "That's what's great about you." He placed his palms over her ears and inclined her head toward his. This time it was a real kiss, his warm tongue searching hers, his arms drawing her in. His lips traced the surface of her face in the night shadows.

She couldn't say what they talked about, or even if they'd continued talking. She had surrendered to elation.

However improbable, Adam Pearl liked her.

13

"Miss Kingsley," Mr. Hissle said, "show the group your spiccato." Turning to the other members of the viola quintet, he said, "The spiccato sets the tempo in the Mozart G Minor. That 'TA-ta-ta-ta' is the first movement's engine. Bouncing your bow is no good with sloppy rhythm. Note that Miss Kingsley has bounce *and* rhythm."

Isaac's insistence on pinging and flicking, circling at the bow's frog and tip, was paying off.

At Penn, Dara went to classes and studied. It was hard to find the hours, but she made practicing a priority. She warmed up with long bow strokes that slowed time and filled her head with sound as fat as she could craft. She heard Isaac's raspy voice telling jokes, urging her to work harder, to concentrate more, to plump up her sound. She was so busy, she hardly noticed him spacing her lessons apart to every two weeks.

14

Good thing my brother is away at college, or he'd prob-ably act like a moron," Dara said to Adam as they stepped off the Paoli local. "My parents will make up for it. They'll ask you a lot of dumb questions."

"Pretty neighborhood," Adam said. He looked at the stone houses lining the street. Dara's neighborhood was nothing like the city. Tall, leafy trees shaded the sidewalks. Houses had drive-ways with cars, sometimes two or three. Adam's parents didn't own a car. "Looks like a movie set," he said.

"Adam, have you heard anything I said?"

"That you'll die of embarrassment the minute I step in the door?" Amused at her nervousness, he brushed a strand of hair from her face. "I didn't realize I was that bad." He took her chin and kissed her. She smelled like rosemary. "Don't worry. I'll try to behave myself."

Mrs. Kingsley was wearing jeans and sneakers; she had just come in from raking leaves. She was taller than Dara, with cropped gray hair. Adam thought of his mother, dressed for work. She never practiced in casual clothes, which meant she never wore them.

"Oreos?" Mrs. Kingsley said. She put a box of orange juice on the table and took out a glass. "Help yourself." Dara rolled her eyes. "If you're anything like Dara's older brother, Rick, who's away at college, you're eating your parents out of house and home."

Adam didn't know what to say. Bella cooked and shopped for the Pearls. Adam's parents did little more than boil water or put a slice of bread in the toaster. Adam wasn't allowed to eat his family "out of house and home." Bella may have spoiled him, but she didn't shop for him. She was employed by his parents.

Mrs. Kingsley hovered over pots and pans, chatting while she cooked. "Do you have brothers or sisters, Adam?"

"No, it's just me and my parents." Adam wasn't used to explaining how he fit in. His family was a threesome, his parents a duet that formed the base of a triangle. As soon as he had the thought, Adam realized how odd this formulation was. The geometry was a means to set themselves apart; his family's certainty was self-congratulatory and unappealing. He looked around Dara's kitchen: papers piled below the beige wall phone; battered cookbooks—bindings taped to keep their covers from falling off—leaning haphazardly on a shelf by the phone; a small frying pan soaking in the sink (a fried egg from breakfast, maybe?); dishes askew in the drainboard and stacked on the counter waiting to be loaded into the dishwasher.

"Mom, I told you!" Dara said.

Adam touched Dara's thigh under the table to signal he felt comfortable here. With Bella's vigilance, nothing was ever out of place in the Pearls' kitchen. The counters were bare other than Adele's small black purse in a corner by the door, waiting for her to snatch it as she ran out for the day.

"I hear your parents are musicians," Mrs. Kingsley said.

"Yes," Adam said. "Pianists." He couldn't recall meeting an adult who wasn't familiar with them, who wasn't awestruck by their accomplishments. Even his grade school teachers had treated him like the son of celebrities. At Dara's he was judged for himself, a young man dating the Kingsleys' daughter, no more and no less. It was liberating.

"Nice to meet you, Adam." Mr. Kingsley strode into the kitchen. Adam stood to shake his hand. "You've certainly got an enthusiastic advance team," Mr. Kingsley said in a ho-ho-ho kind of voice.

"Dad!"

"Don't stand on my account," Mr. Kingsley boomed. He was tall and bald, eyes the same color as Dara's, his handshake firm. Adam wondered what Christmas morning was like at the Kingsleys'. He pictured them around a tree they'd decorated together, torn wrapping paper on the floor that no one hurried to clean up, the smell of mulled cider, and Mr. Kingsley making waffles. Christmas wasn't much in Adam's house. His father, who was Jewish—if lapsed—hadn't grown up with it.

"You'll have to excuse me," Mr. Kingsley said. "One of the sinks upstairs is leaking, and we'll have a flood if I don't get to the hardware store." He threw on a coat.

"Pick up a card for Aunt Sally's birthday, will you?" Mrs. Kingsley said to Mr. Kingsley, who didn't so much walk as lope out.

Dara showed Adam around the house. He stood at the door to her bedroom, afraid Mrs. Kingsley would disapprove if he went in. Dara told him that she had chosen the shiny white desk with the curved legs in second grade when her mother redecorated her room.

"Ah, the piles of books," Adam said. He stared at the ruffled pink bedspread. "So, this is where you sleep."

"I feel like I'm seeing the room for the first time," Dara said. "It's for a little girl, isn't it? Embarrassing." Her bulletin board had several troll dolls hanging by their blue hair, and three or four gaudy Mardi Gras necklaces looped over a nail. Dara looked as if she could cry. "Blech, I hate you seeing this. We better go downstairs."

Over plates of stuffed ziti and garlic bread, Mr. Kingsley said, "Adam, you must be hitting the books. I think you're the same age as Dara's older brother, Rick. He's at Penn State. Maybe she told you."

"Dad!"

"That's great, Mr. Kingsley," Adam said.

"He likes it there," Mrs. Kingsley said. "He seems to be applying himself to his studies. Finally."

"College is hard work," Adam agreed. He didn't want to disabuse Dara's parents about life at Caldwell. There weren't books; there were scores, lots of them. There weren't study hours; there were days of endless practice. He didn't mention these points for fear the Kingsleys would think less of him. He wanted them to like him. In fact, he really wanted them to like him.

Adam sat in the semicircle around Maxim Gordofsky, the violin student chosen to play for Ruggiero Ricci's master class. Maxim, a third-year student at Caldwell, had daunting pyrotechnics. He laid into the first Paganini Caprice at a tempo Adam knew was unsustainable. Rosin dust smoked from Maxim's bow as he broke chords like a bucking bronco. Adam was motion sick at the speed of his attack. Was this music or performance Olympics?

Ricci waved his bow for Maxim to stop. "Nice bow technique, young man," he said. Maxim's face was covered in sweat. "But your left hand. You're going to cramp, if not now, then as you get older," Ricci cautioned. "And God help you if you do it in performance. You have your instrument in a stranglehold. Put your violin over your head and take a stretch." Ricci tapped the left side of Maxim's neck with the tip of his bow. Turning to the students in the surrounding semicircle, he said, "See the tension in those muscles? We can feel it in the music." Maxim looked crestfallen.

The young woman to Adam's left poked him and whispered, "What the hell was that?"

"A car race?" How much performance at Caldwell was simply showing off?

"Loosen your grip!" Ricci said. Maxim started up at half speed as Ricci made comments about his left wrist and thumb.

As he watched Maxim harness his inner demons, Adam wondered what Dara was doing. Adam envied her enthusiasm about her studies. She was always caught up in something—a class, or a research paper. He pictured her surrounded by hordes of students who could swallow her up and leave Adam on the outside looking in. He wished he could see her more.

Ricci stopped Maxim again and shook out Maxim's left wrist. "I said, loosen up, young man!"

"Where are your parents this week?" Dara asked, as Adam opened the door to the Pearls' apartment.

"Do we have to talk about them?" Adam hung her coat in the hall closet. "Salzburg, then Graz and Vienna, I think."

"You've met my family," Dara said, following him into the living room. The piano keyboards were closed, but the lids remained open, poised for the Pearls' return. "My dad gets excited about the latest biography of Teddy Roosevelt. There's no music. Let's not even mention my brother, Rick." Adam looked halfway between annoyed and glum. She pressed on. "Your parents are so exotic."

"You don't see what I see. I'm invisible, especially to my mother," Adam said, exasperated. "The whole building fills with their piano playing. They go over every measure, every dynamic marking, every phrase, a thousand times. I may as well not be here," he said. "My mother travels to a different place; she's not on earth."

"You're not invisible!" Dara was taken aback by his outburst, blistering and unfamiliar. She felt a strange need to protect him. "I'm here!" she said, as if declaring her presence would help. He seemed sure of himself, whereas she suffered from insecurities surrounding her studies and her playing. But not regarding her family. They just were.

"When I was younger," Adam said slowly, "I figured their practicing and ignoring me was meant to prepare me for their trips. I'd lie under my mother's piano while she banged it out, just to be close to her."

Dara was tearful at this image. "Which piano is hers?"

He pointed to the far end of the living room.

"Come here!" Dara took Adam's hand, maneuvered around the pianos, and crawled under Adele's, pulling Adam on top of her. "Let me hold you." She couldn't believe the weight of him. His legs were like stone columns. She ran her palm over his head and down his back, resting it on his rear. "Was I mean, wanting to hear about your parents?"

"Mean?" He lifted his head. "No, not mean." There was something he seemed to want to add but didn't.

They kissed for a long, slow while.

He rolled over next to her. "I doubt they had a plan for me," he said, picking up the thread of conversation. "They weren't intentionally training me for their absences. They just get overtaken by music, in thrall to each other. You'll hear them. They have a concert at Caldwell when they come back. Maybe you'll come?" he said, staring up at his mother's soundboard.

"When you talk about your parents, it sounds lonely for you," Dara said.

He closed his eyes and squeezed her hand. "Maybe so."

Dara followed Adam through the dining room, shelves lined with musical scores, down the hall. His parents' room came first, with a wall of records, a huge sound system, and a bed. Then their study. Signed photographs on the walls of musicians and conductors from around the world were hung above two mahogany desks. One was empty, the other piled with correspondence. "My mother goes through her letters faster than my father," Adam commented.

Adam's bedroom was a smaller version of his parents', the floor covered in a Persian rug, and shelves filled with music and recordings. His twin bed was pushed against the wall to make room for a music stand. He had a stereo with earphones to study scores while his parents practiced. A picture of Yuri Zablonsky with his arm around Adam hung on the wall, signed *To my favorite violinist, Yuri Z.*

"How old are you in this picture?" Dara asked. "Ten?"

"Nine. I have an idea," Adam said, selecting a record and dropping the needle in the middle of the disk. "Brahms Piano

Quartet, Op. 60. You have to hear the slow movement. Brahms wrote this for the great love of his life, Clara Schumann."

Dara sat on his bed, immersed in warm, lyrical cello sound, the piano in respectful accompaniment. The violin entered; the cello dipped to minor. Were the instruments crying or singing? "I can't believe I've lived my whole life without hearing this."

Adam laughed. "You mean all eighteen years?"

She held up her hands and spread her fingers. "Do you think I could play it?"

"Of course!"

She studied her hands. The tip of her right thumb was dented and black with the patina rubbed off the leather band at the base of her bow. The second finger on her right hand had a callus between the knuckles. In that tiny expanse was leverage for the dynamic range of her instrument. The veins of both her hands protruded prominently from practicing.

On the recording, the viola entered with a deep brown sound.

Dara's hands had become powerful, muscular. Each left-hand finger possessed a force of its own, its own personality. The more she bore into a precise spot on the string, the more intense the sound. "Gorgeous viola part," she said.

"The viola was Brahms's love language to Clara," Adam said.

Adam's fingers were supple and graceful plying the fingerboard. His hands were athletic and deft. Dara admired his willowy fingers. But his touch on her skin was something else altogether, as he unraveled her braid, found her under her black sweater and caressed the inside of her thigh.

He wore the same rapt expression making love as when he played violin. He traced her body with his long fingers and her nipples with the swirl of his warm tongue.

There must be no bigger place than his narrow bed.

He let himself in—carefully—his forehead touching hers.

They rocked together and held each other and slept. At

dusk, Dara awoke to Adam's whisper. "We better get dressed before Bella shows up."

Adam felt the futility of being alone when he turned out the light in his bedroom that night. Where should he put the caring that welled up in him? He would rather she had slept over. He would rather have held her in the dark, would rather his parents stayed away.

Was it worse to have felt her body? Worse that she'd left her naked impression in his twin bed? She had named the ungainly creature that had inhabited his chest since childhood. *Loneliness.* What was he supposed to do with that?

15

Adam finished teaching and headed down to the Caldwell office to check his mail.

"Mr. Pearl, you'd better take a look." Mrs. Grant pulled out a sheet of paper. "That's who wants to come to your mother's memorial."

It was a list with dozens, maybe hundreds, of names, written in Mrs. Grant's sloped, regular hand. "Are you still thinking of a concert?" she asked. "Because Lord knows we aren't going to fit this many people in Caldwell Hall."

Adam leafed through Mrs. Grant's list, page after page. "I can't believe there are so many names," Adam said. Whatever he had expected, it wasn't this.

"The phone's been ringing off the hook. Everyone loved your mother. She was so kind."

Was she? Adam stacked the papers. *Professor Dara Kingsley, University of Pennsylvania.* Twenty-first on the list, at the bottom of the first page.

"Did all these people call?" he asked. He handed the pile back to Mrs. Grant, his face growing warm.

"Like I said, Mr. Pearl, the phone's been ringing off the hook. I can make a spreadsheet for a mailing, but I was waiting to see what you wanted. I don't want to bother your father."

"Thanks, don't bother him. We'll have to find another venue," Adam said, more to himself than to her. He was shaken to see Dara's name on the list.

"That's what I'm saying, Mr. Pearl. You can't fit all those people in here, even if half of them don't show. Independence Theatre might work."

"Wonderful idea," he said, grateful for her practicality.

The concert would have to be grander, more formal than

Adam had envisioned. He'd imagined an intimate Sunday afternoon at Caldwell, performers dressed in shirtsleeves instead of tuxedos. The opportunity for audience members to reminisce. He'd hoped to hear stories about his mother, maybe find a new angle on her. He would have to shift his thinking to concert formals and engraved invitations. A press kit for music critics. It dawned on him that his mother would have been pleased by the Independence Theatre. She loved Caldwell, but she loved the glare of the lights more.

Dara's name was on the list. Her life must be very different from the one he'd known, with her husband and academic career. She might be entirely unrecognizable—plenty of people were after two decades. What would she think of Adam if she met him now? Living a block away from his parents, teaching at Caldwell, following the career they'd set out.

Well, not quite. Adam would never fulfill his mother's ambitions.

16

What's with Phillip Hissle?" Adam asked Victor as he opened a bag of sandwich bread in his father's kitchen. "He's been following me around."

"He must miss your mother."

"I don't think I ever had a conversation with him before she died."

"Phillip was always friendly to her, in his strange way," Victor said, opening the cabinet to retrieve plates.

"He said something about you not letting Mother accompany him in a recital."

Victor laughed. "Me? I doubt she had any interest in accompanying him. Or anyone else for that matter. She was all about two pianos. Could you put mustard on mine, please?" He handed Adam the plates and pulled out a chair. "On the other hand, there were things she didn't share."

"Like what?"

"I made the mistake of wandering into the study at two a.m. last night," Victor said. "I've forgotten how to sleep. Every day I get more and more mail. Invitations for us to teach at summer music festivals. They don't even realize she's gone. I was such a fractured mess that in the middle of the night I figured that I'd talk it over with her in the morning." He sighed.

The telephone rang. "Sid Gellman to tune the pianos? Sure, let him up." Victor hung up. "I didn't know he was coming. Your mother must have scheduled the appointment months ago."

"I'll let you visit with Sid, Dad," Adam said, giving his father a hug. "You're going to be okay," he added, though he had no idea how.

☙

Victor followed Sid into the living room. The stack of music on Adele's piano was as she'd left it. "Awfully sorry about Mrs. Pearl's passing," Sid said. "Gad, she was a great lady."

"Tea or a glass of water, Sid?" Victor asked.

"A cup of tea would hit the spot, Mr. Pearl."

"I wouldn't have half my clients if it weren't for Mrs. Pearl," Sid said. "She phoned her friends when I was just starting out, to tell them to hire me. She made it happen."

Victor went into the kitchen and put on the kettle for their tea. Adele had been the one who joined Sid in the living room when he visited, swapping notes about Sid's clientele. She was fascinated by Sid's latest electronic device. It had a pitch memory for recording the idiosyncrasies of each piano he tuned. Sid was the only one Adele trusted to work on her instrument, and she insisted on the same loving attention toward Victor's. She'd show Sid that Victor's low B flat was out of tune, or that the notes in the upper registers had slipped. "Sid," she'd say, "don't forget to check the humidity measurement."

"Can't do anything about the heat in this building, can you, Mrs. Pearl?" The same exchange, every time.

Victor brought in Sid's tea. "Shall I work on Mrs. Pearl's piano today?" Sid asked.

"Of course," Victor replied, astonished he'd ask such a question.

Again! In that brief moment, Victor had forgotten that his wife was dead. He retreated to the kitchen and pounded his fist on the kitchen table. Adele hadn't stepped out to run over to Caldwell. Every little thing reminded Victor of what was missing. The clink of her teacup in its saucer as she chatted with Sid; the slant of her body as she leaned against the living room wall, one foot extended, her head slightly tilted, overseeing the inspection of her prized instrument. Here was poor Sid Gellman, loyally performing his duties, stirring up an emotional tempest. It was unbearable.

Sid's hands traveled in arpeggios up and down the keyboard,

chord combinations peculiar to the piano tuner. As they grew louder and more complex, Victor realized just how quiet the apartment had become.

Sid was checking the highest octaves; he would be finished soon. It was time for Adele to push open the kitchen door and say how reassured she was that her instrument was in good hands.

❧

Adam opened the glass door to the Caldwell library. The New Philadelphia Trio may not have completed this year's season, but Adam was looking ahead to the next. "What have you got?" he asked the librarian.

She handed him several scores with accompanying CDs. "Also, Anton Krusak asked if you would try this," she said, handing him another CD and score. "As a new member of the composition faculty, he's anxious to hear his pieces performed."

"Thanks," Adam said. "I'll have a listen." He headed to the bank of CD players. Hissle was seated at the right end of the row with a headset on. Adam felt like kicking him. Maybe he should come back another day for the Krusak. On the other hand, why should he be defeated by Hissle, whoever he was, whatever he'd done? Adam reorganized his stack of music and sat down at a CD player. He put on a set of headphones and slid Krusak's CD into the slot.

The music began with discordant, twanging plucking from the violin and cello, followed by a lyrical piano line. The parts didn't fit together.

He skipped to Krusak's second movement. This time the three instruments started together. No harmony, just a mind-numbing series of notes in unison that sounded more like the soundtrack for a horror movie than a piano trio. If there was any promise to the piece at all, it wouldn't be apparent today.

Adam walked back to the librarian. "Mind if I take the Krusak home? Maybe the other stuff too?"

"No problem, Mr. Pearl. I'll fill out a card for you."

Adam started to leave but changed his mind. He turned around, walked back to the CD players, and pulled up a chair next to Hissle. "Phillip," he said, before he had time to organize his thoughts.

Hissle looked up.

"What was it between you and my mother?"

Hissle wrinkled his forehead in puzzlement. He hadn't taken off his earphones.

Adam reached over and ripped the headset off. "I said, what was it between you and my mother?"

Hissle pursed his lips and squinted. "Nobody could feel about her the way I did." He retrieved his earphones, put them back on, and calmly turned up the volume.

Adam stood to go. "I guess my father doesn't count."

17

Dara cocked her head as they stepped out of the elevator. Piano music blanketed the hall. "Adam, can we stay out here and listen?"

"You mean the French Suites? My mother's playing the whole set in a couple of weeks. It's okay to go in; she won't stop because we're here. She's working even harder for her solo recital than she does with my dad."

Dara sat transfixed in the Pearls' kitchen, afraid that if she moved, Adele would cease her alchemy. The kitchen clock ticked the seconds going by, but Dara was oblivious to the passage of time. The Pearls' apartment, which up to now had felt like hers and Adam's alone, had been transformed, piano playing infusing it like incense in a temple.

At the finale to the third suite, Adele came into the kitchen, shaking out her hands. Forty-five minutes had gone by, but for Dara it could have been either a whole day or a blink of an eye.

"How are you, dear?" Adele said to Dara, as if she had just returned from a trip to the grocery store. "How was your morning, Adam? Your Schumann rehearsal? Does your trio sound good?" Without waiting for an answer, she wiped her forehead with a wet paper towel. "Time for the next three," she said, striding past them. "Dad should be home soon." She set upon the fourth French Suite, arpeggiated harmonies drifting from the living room.

"Is this what it's always like?" Dara said.

"You mean all she does is practice?"

"I would be paralyzed living this close to perfection."

"Nobody's perfect. Especially my mother."

Dara touched his cheek. She liked the feel of his stubble, the fact that she could tell how long ago he'd shaved. She felt his

anger, cloaked in cynicism, and leaned forward to press her lips
to his forehead. She wished she could dissipate his tension. "I
don't know how you do it," she said. "I couldn't practice here.
I'd be a wreck hearing my mistakes. It's already hard enough."

"Don't say that to my mother. She'll go into her practice
rant. How work is the only thing that matters, blah, blah, blah."

"How did you ever learn to play violin?"

"You mean despite my mother shouting that my F sharps
were high, or that I should lean into my bow? It's just how it
was. Is. You heard her questions about my trio. She wants us to
go professional; she has agents lined up for us. Christ, I've got
another two years before I graduate Caldwell. Do I even want
that?"

"Do you?" Dara asked. The track he was on seemed natural
for him.

"I figure that's what I'll do," Adam said. "I never thought
about it much. Until I met you."

She was surprised. "Why?"

The kitchen door swung open, and Victor greeted Dara.
"Cup of tea?"

Adele appeared. "Victor, you boiled the water? Why, thank
you!" she said, pulling up a chair. "I need to refuel. Dara, how
are your studies with Isaac going?"

"He's wonderful."

"Do you practice?"

"Mother!" Adam protested. "Of course she practices."

"I could always do more," Dara added. "But freshman
coursework takes up a lot of time."

"Didn't Isaac want you to go to the conservatory?"

"Yes," Dara said. "But my parents wouldn't let me." She
shouldn't have said it. The Pearls' every day began and ended
with music; they wouldn't understand. She searched for a way
to redeem herself.

"It's a shame Isaac is sick," Adele said.

"What?" Dara looked from Adele to Adam.

Dara felt chilled recalling the gauntness in Isaac's face, how tired he'd been lately. He had even spaced her lessons out every two weeks. She'd seen it but hadn't admitted it to herself.

"At some point he'll have to cut back," Adele said.

"What's wrong with him?" Dara asked, unsettled by her obliviousness.

"Rumor is that it's either throat or mouth cancer," Victor said. "But that's conjecture. Isaac hasn't said anything."

Isaac's pipe was so much a part of who he was.

"Dara, let's go out," Adam said.

"How did I not see it?" Dara said, stomping out of the elevator. "Is mouth cancer a big deal?" She knew the answer. "Adam! You've known all along and said nothing?"

"What difference would it have made?" Adam said.

"Don't patronize me! He's like a grandfather to me. I adore him. I won't get anywhere without him." As she said it, she realized Adam couldn't understand, couldn't imagine the precarity of her musical life, her fear that her hard work might not get her where she desperately wanted to go.

They walked around Rittenhouse Square, as if clocking laps. Adam tried to hug her. She pulled back, glaring at him. Where was her future?

"It's supposed to be good to study with a range of teachers," he said. "I had to beat back my parents to turn down Juilliard. They wanted me to be exposed to a different teaching style from Yuri's, but I said no."

"Poor baby," Dara said, furious. "Had to turn down Juilliard." She picked up the pace. "You'll get to do whatever you want, and you know it. It's not the same for me. I come from nothing musically. Nothing is a given."

"Now do you get it?" Adam said. "My mother can be awful. You shouldn't pay attention to her."

"I'm not talking about your mother! You didn't think to let me know about Isaac, damn you." She shoved her sleeve up to check her watch. "I'll see you. I have work to do."

"You think you're the first one to have a fight with your boyfriend?" Lily said over the phone. She and Dara had frequent calls once they started school, Lily at Juilliard and Dara at Penn.

"Of course not." Dara wanted comfort, not a talking-to.

"If you could only see the cesspool in New York. I got 'christened' by some guy I didn't even know. Good riddance to him."

"Jesus, Lils. What happened?"

"We're talking about you right now. You had a fight. Big shit."

"Are you okay?"

"Like I said, this one's about you. I'll tell you about it next time you're in New York," Lily said. "Fortunately, I'm not going to bump into him anytime soon. I've moved on."

It didn't sound like she'd moved on. "Lily, stop. Talk to me."

"It was a one-night stand. I didn't care to give him any personal details. It's better that way. Hurt like hell. Not worth going into."

"Lils," Dara said quietly. "This is serious. Are you getting help? Can I do anything?"

"Dara, shut up already! I shouldn't have said anything. You want to hear the real problem? My teacher is a sadist. That would be Katherine Rhodes, piano faculty at the Juilliard School. She throws books at the Asian students when she wakes up on the wrong side of the bed. She practically brained Jeff Chang the other day. She hasn't done it to me yet, but she will. She's vicious." Lily lowered her voice. "Dara, I thought I had been around the block, but I've never seen cruelty like this. I hurt like hell from tendonitis, and I don't think I can practice any harder."

Dara started to suggest Lily see a doctor but thought better of it. Lily would say it was bougie crap.

"When Katherine Rhodes was twenty-nine, she had a memory lapse playing with the New York Phil," Lily said. "Got lost in the middle of the first movement of the 'Emperor' concerto. Walked offstage, came back with her music, and finished the concert without someone to turn pages. So, she's turning her own pages, ripping them as she goes, dropping notes, getting more and more frantic. Can you imagine? Every musician's nightmare. Supposedly, she was 'a rising star.' She never played in public again. For this, she was rewarded with a full-time piano faculty position at Juilliard. She's been taking it out on students ever since."

"Lily, you have to change teachers!" Dara thought of her dorm room at Penn, her nice-enough roommates, the meals provided, her parents' regular tuition payments, and what she stressed over—finishing her reading, finding time to practice, and too many papers. And Adam. Could her concerns be more trivial? And Isaac.

"What the hell are you smoking?" Lily said. "Katherine won't even let us go to master classes with other teachers. I doubt I'd graduate if I tried."

"Lily!"

"Forget about it, Dara. Let's get back to you." Lily's wicked humor masked more pressure than Dara could understand. "C'mon, spit it out."

"Why didn't Adam tell me Isaac was sick?" Dara wished she hadn't called.

"Maybe he wasn't thinking about you every second of the day, dreamy-eyes. Maybe he was trying to spare you getting upset."

"I hate that."

"Tell him."

"I don't want to see him right now."

"So, don't. But I suspect this is about Isaac."

Dara started to cry.

"I get it," Lily said. "Isaac is funnier and nicer than anyone else. Plus, his students get good jobs. You should see the garbage at Juilliard. And not just Katherine. Half the teachers are either vindictive or deadwood. Or you don't get anywhere unless you sleep with them." She sighed. "Honey. Welcome to reality. At least you have a nice boyfriend."

"That's what I can't stand," Dara sobbed.

Whiplashed, Adam hurried west on Market past Thirtieth Street Station. He was cutting into his practice time, but so be it. It was true; he'd overheard his parents discussing Isaac's illness and had withheld it from Dara. It was an indictment, an acceptance of the way things worked at home. He'd been raised on discretion. His parents insisted that nothing they shared about other musicians be repeated beyond their walls. Adam hadn't questioned their rules. Shame on him. He shouldn't mindlessly follow their protocols. He should forge his own path.

Students from Penn and Drexel crowded the streets, laughing and carrying backpacks. It was as if they—and Dara—were from another country, the country of normal. Dara would interpret that as an insult, but Adam meant the opposite. What a contrast to Caldwell's plush rooms, where music came through every door. He was living in the rarefied atmosphere of elite musicians and resented every minute of it.

Red-eyed, Dara opened the door to her dorm room, her hair falling out of her braid. A half-eaten bag of popcorn lay on the floor. Adam heard girls laughing from one of the bedrooms adjoining the common space.

"May I come in?" he asked.

"Let's go out," she said. "Too many people around."

"I've upset you," he said.

"It doesn't take a genius to figure that out," she said. They sat on a bench in the quad. "I can't believe you didn't tell me."

"I should have."

"Yes, you should have. I don't want to be protected. Ever."

18

Yvette motioned Dara into her office and closed the door. "I have news," she said, lowering her voice. "Carmen's pregnant! We're out of the first trimester."

"That's fantastic!" Dara said, giving Yvette a hug. "Can I be an auntie?"

"You don't have to ask. It's been a saga."

"Wait, for how long? Why didn't you tell me?"

"Too superstitious. Too nervous. Besides, you've been a little preoccupied."

"I need to hear everything." Yvette's announcement made Dara's worries seem petty.

"Keep your fingers crossed or say your prayers or whatever you do," Yvette said.

"How is Carmen feeling?"

"She's done throwing up, which is exciting. For her, especially. She was so sick she started losing weight. I think that's over."

"Sounds nasty. And stressful. Tell her congratulations! The second trimester is supposed to be easier. What kind of baby are you having?"

"Human, I hope. We're down for the surprise. The whole thing's surreal anyway."

"I'm thrilled for you. I gotta say, I feel further from that than at any time in my life. I need to abandon the whole coupling enterprise." She hoped she wasn't taking away from Yvette's moment.

"Sit down and talk sense, will you?"

"I love what you and Carmen have," Dara said, pulling up a chair. "You're both so sane."

"That's not the highest standard."

"I had the big wedding, the luscious orchid bouquet, the

exotic honeymoon in Thailand, the husband who was a 'great catch,' and look where it landed me."

"I won't comment about men being an inferior class of human, or that they need to re-evolve to somewhere a lot better. Or that testosterone is the source of most of what's bad in the world, and that if we don't smash the patriarchy we'll keep limping along, or else drive straight off a cliff." Yvette grinned.

"Glad you refrained from expressing your opinion," Dara said. "And I agree with you, by the way, which may sound odd coming from a cis white woman."

"Ha ha."

"Yvette," Dara said, "I'm so happy for you. Keep me posted!"

Dara headed down the hall to her office, surprised to feel regret. Did Dara want children? She had been ambivalent even before she awoke to the man she'd married. Thank the powers that be that she hadn't had Matt's baby; warfare over a child would be untenable. Their endless divorce, dragging on like Jarndyce v. Jarndyce, was bad enough. What were they fighting over anyway? Matt was after some all-encompassing victory—so he could pose triumphant in a sweaty boxing ring, his foot on Dara's limp body? Her best bet was to close the lid on romantic attachments.

She hoped Yvette wouldn't get ground down like other mothers among Dara's colleagues. When their child was sick or their nanny walked out, they hid behind closed doors or snuck out in the middle of the day. They arrived later than intended to faculty meetings and checked their phones too often. They worked like demons, faces drawn from lack of sleep, huddled around the coffeemaker when one more mother was forced from the academy. Yvette had tenure and a steady disposition, coupled with a fierce determination to make things work. No, Yvette would be fine.

19

Adam and Dara went to Adele's solo Bach concert at Bryn Mawr College. Adam stayed close to Dara and introduced her to the musical illuminati as his girlfriend.

They attended the Pearls' next concert at Caldwell, a trial run before the Pearls' London–Leeds–Edinburgh tour. Adam held Dara as if she belonged, as if they were a couple, which—incredibly—they were.

Pearl and Pearl left on tour.

Adam's magical bedroom, where Dara was enveloped in joy. With his parents away, Dara could ignore how intimidating they were. She could push aside her fears about music and luxuriate in the feeling that it was right with Adam; that his palm on her hip, his lips on her breast, were pleasures as natural as the color green after a rainstorm. She didn't want their nights to end, their cocoon to open.

Dara finished her freshman year.

Then she was a sophomore and Adam a senior.

He practiced in his room with her cross-legged on his bed, surrounded by books. She would look up to see him disappear into music of his own making, smiling at her when he reemerged.

Sometimes she had the sense that he was playing for her, and it felt very good.

"What is it today?" he would ask.

"John Locke, political theory," Dara would say. Or, "Paleontology. Science isn't my strong suit; I'm taking it pass/fail. The professor is so excited about dinosaurs that he makes it exciting for everyone else." Or, "Greek history. Herodotus turns out to be a page-turner."

"I thought you were an English major."

"I have to take advantage of what's out there, don't I?"

He nodded.

"It's never too late," she said. "You could study other stuff."

"I've never seen anyone make it work."

"What about me?" It was an enormous undertaking to make time to practice. "It's hard to keep all the balls in the air," she said, sighing as she answered her own question. "Never mind. You're meant to play violin. The world needs your music."

In October came the hideous news of Isaac's death. His huge hands, each finger a big round paddle, were stilled. The fingertips on his right hand, perennially blackened by pipe tobacco and garden dirt, gone. His fat, creamy sound was silenced.

Dara had not been able to conceive of Isaac dying, despite watching him waste away. She loved him too much to imagine a world without him. He'd taken her under his wing; she'd hung her musical destiny on him. He was supposed to place her in an orchestra and ensure her musical success. Her future was suddenly fragile, collapsed under his absence.

She couldn't unclench her fists to touch her fingerboard or hold her bow. She curled up on her dormitory bed—a tense ball—and wept.

As soon as Mrs. Koroff opened the door to their modest row house, Dara burst into tears. "Come in, darling," the white-haired Mrs. Koroff said. "It's never good to cry by yourself."

"Thank you."

The Koroffs' living room had a sofa and two armchairs upholstered in green velvet, crowded together by a baby grand piano. Four music stands were positioned in the corner for Caldwell String Quartet rehearsals.

Isaac's viola lay under the piano, a dog that had lost its master. "I've never seen Mr. Koroff's case closed," Dara said, weeping.

They sat together on the couch. Mrs. Koroff put her arm around Dara and shared the story of how Isaac got his start. "His mama bought him a violin, bow, case, stand, and music book, all for five dollars and twenty-five cents. Don't you know he'd rather be playing baseball, not practicing? His papa was furious at the waste of money. But his mother said he had talent because he followed the hurdy-gurdy man around the neighborhood. It turned out that the attraction was the hurdy-gurdy man's monkey! Isaac didn't give a hoot about the music. It was dumb luck that his mama's forcing him to practice paid off."

Mrs. Koroff prattled on. "Want to know how to compliment a musician after a poor performance?"

"Sure."

"I go to enough terrible concerts; I've developed a list," Mrs. Koroff said. "'What a performance!' 'I've never heard the piece played that way!'" She winked at Dara. "There's usually a reason why a piece is 'the infrequently played.'" Dara laughed through her tears.

Mrs. Koroff squeezed her hand. "Go on with your studies, dear. Isaac thought the world of you."

20

Victor awoke knowing today was something big. He lay in bed trying to remember what it was. Chopin Nocturnes played in his head like distant echoes. Solo piano music had broken the oppressive silence. Half of him was gone.

He'd promised to return to his students today. That was it. Saturday mornings at Caldwell. The children.

Once, he believed he'd mastered the Nocturnes. He'd played them for his senior recital at Juilliard. He recalled his teacher urging him to play more expressively without rendering the music pedestrian, or worse, melodramatic.

What was his Saturday morning routine? Toast, that was it. He adjusted his tie and wandered into the kitchen.

At Juilliard, Victor had had a reputation as an intellectual pianist. "Pencil Hands," they called him, for his long hours in the music library dandling a pencil, comparing scores or researching the history of pieces he was learning.

He opened the door to the refrigerator. The orange marmalade was almost empty. Without Adele reminding him, he'd have to remember to buy more on the way home from Caldwell.

How little Victor had understood in his student days! His unabashed confidence, his drive to succeed. In Adele's orbit, he'd grown up. *Victor, all the studying in the world isn't going to fix the ensemble here, not if our phrasing isn't together.* No matter how he prepared each piece and investigated its origins, Adele expanded him, pushed his musical thinking beyond himself.

Adele's illness extended him differently; Victor became nurse and comforter. She wouldn't have stood for it if she'd been well. As the music left her, she said things he'd never heard. "I've been leaning on you my whole life," she said one afternoon. "I just didn't know it."

It might have been easier to have remained that young man at Juilliard, ignoring time's whimsy. Now time elongated and compressed. That boy at Juilliard felt as immediate as whatever Victor was now—an aging widower, he supposed.

Time was everything to a musician, the driving structure behind music, even more than melody or harmony. Like a building's foundation, the importance of time was evident only with a flaw in its execution—a performer who rushed or dragged the tempo or took rhythmic liberties that violated the composition's spirit.

Then there was the time it took to practice; maintaining technique was a daily obligation. And new repertoire, which had to be acquired with enough time to embed it in the fingers so that by performance it was second nature.

What about professional time? Only a child would consider arriving at rehearsal as the conductor dropped his first downbeat. Musicians knew the importance of coming to rehearsals early enough to squeeze in last-minute practice, and to concerts with ample time to warm up.

Despite the breakneck speed of the past decades, time was at a standstill. And yet. Victor checked his watch. Time to go. He closed the door to his apartment and pressed the elevator button. He was teaching five students from the preparatory division today, all under the age of twelve. That was Pearl and Pearl's way; Victor took the youngest children—the prodigies—and handed them over to Adele when they reached their late teens. Prodigies existed in a dangerous limbo; if they were pushed too hard or otherwise mishandled, they burnt out. Or worse, became mentally unstable.

Children tended to be eager and fresh faced, ears wide open. Ants in their pants and music at their fingertips. Victor would go through the motions. Maybe they would be his ticket back to some kind of being. Hadn't his whole life taught him the value of repetition?

Today's first pupil was Svetlana Eglevsky, the seven-year-old daughter of Russian immigrants. Her mother took extraordinary care to dress her for lessons. Each week Svetlana came with her flaxen hair pulled into a tight ponytail. Victor never understood how she could blink. Svetlana wore smock dresses with sashes; lacy, cuffed ankle socks; and patent-leather Mary Janes.

Svetlana's mother, whose English was halting, normally bowed and smiled through gold-capped teeth when she saw Victor. Today she held both his hands in hers and wept. "Mr. Pearl, so sorry, so sorry! Mrs. Pearl so good, so kind. So sorry!" Victor wished he could speak Russian so he could beg her to stop. He would never make it through Svetlana's lesson if he broke down.

Svetlana's feet didn't reach the pedals. She swung her legs back and forth and wrinkled her forehead in concentration. She was working on a Bach partita. "Mr. Pearl, will you play it for me?"

Victor hadn't opened a keyboard since Adele died.

Svetlana looked up at him with an expectant grin. Sliding down the piano bench to make room, she folded her hands in her lap.

And he played! He made it through the whole movement. Strains of Bach filled his studio; Svetlana's excited breathing whistled through the gap where her two front teeth used to be.

When he finished, Victor closed his eyes for a moment of silence. His hands worked; the music had come without effort. He was floating after a long absence from swimming.

"Do you think you can try it now?" he said.

She played his phrases back to him.

The exchange of tunes from one pianist to another, the world that he and Adele had inhabited. What a way to spend your life, tossing phrases from your keyboard to your wife's, hearing them returned, embellished, brightened. Who needed words when you could make music by day, make love by night?

Victor had been afraid to look in a mirror, for fear that having lost his double, his image would have atomized. But here was little Svetlana, too short to reach the pedals, echoing his rendition of the Partita, returning it like a present wrapped in tissue. Victor didn't know how to thank her.

At home, Victor took advantage of this tiny slice of possibility. Before he removed his overcoat, he pasted Adele's obituary into her album and put it back on the shelf.

21

Dara climbed the wooden steps to Phillip Hissle's studio and nodded as he stood sentinel in the doorway. She was so leveled by Isaac Koroff's death that she'd hardly given a thought to her first private lesson with Mr. Hissle. "Our quintet is thinking of getting together to sightread," she said, opening her case and rosining her bow.

No response. Mr. Hissle was not the storyteller Isaac was.

"Do you have suggestions for what we should try?" Dara asked, tuning her instrument.

"Another Mozart," Mr. Hissle said tonelessly.

Mr. Hissle didn't strike Dara as someone who would tolerate hearing her plow through umpteen Ševčík variations the way Isaac had. "I have the first movement of a Marcello sonata prepared," she said. She concentrated on breathing and circular bowing, considered the arrows penciled over the notes in her music, Isaac's phrase markings.

Hearing nothing from Mr. Hissle, Dara plunged in. She was surprised by her nerves; Mr. Hissle was familiar with her playing after months of coaching her in her quintet. He liked her sound; he'd repeatedly asked her to demonstrate her bow technique for the other members of the quintet.

When Dara finished the movement, she put down her viola. Mr. Hissle sat in a folding chair drumming his fingers in his lap. "I think my intonation was off," she ventured. Isaac would have had her warm up first.

"Miss Kingsley, you play like a deaf girl! Didn't Koroff care about whether you were in tune?" Mr. Hissle said in a sudden burst. "You can't have thought that was acceptable. Play it again."

Rattled, Dara lifted her viola. Isaac would never have been so mean, no matter his disappointment. Her second time through was worse; nothing was in tune. Her bow slid around the strings, and she lost hold of the phrasing.

"That's enough for this afternoon. I see no reason to continue," Mr. Hissle said in a venomous whisper. "Find something new to learn for next week; one of the Hindemith pieces for unaccompanied viola will do. They have them in the library here. I'd like some kind of ear when you show up again." He took his post at the doorway, following her out with a cold stare.

Fortunately, Dara was not meeting Adam today. She hoped she wouldn't bump into anyone she knew going up to the library. Especially Cindy Goff, whom Dara now recalled seeing kneeling by her case, weeping after a chamber music coaching. She wondered if Mr. Hissle had ever said anything this awful to Cindy.

Dara signed out the music and headed for the bus, walking toward Rittenhouse Square. What if Adam's parents were looking out their apartment windows? What if Adam was? She couldn't let him find out what Mr. Hissle had said. She would have to keep it a secret, would have to redouble her efforts before her next lesson, and practice longer and harder.

The Hindemith sonata was wickedly difficult, full of double stops. Dissonances challenged her ability to tell whether she was in tune. She took apart each chord, splitting the bottom from the top to firm up the interval in her ear, and worked each finger separately, up and down in alternating rhythms—the way Isaac had taught her—to boost their strength and endurance. She added an extra hour of practice every day after dinner.

Adam called. "I have to practice," she said. She wouldn't see him.

"Hold on, Dara. My parents are back. They asked if you could come for dinner next weekend. We can go out afterward," he added.

She hung up and picked up her instrument. Isaac had said

she was the ninety percent. She shouldn't expect Mr. Hissle to teach her how to do this. She needed to go to her next lesson fully prepared. Trying to channel Isaac, she sharpened a pencil and marked her music.

"What's the matter?" Lily asked on the phone.

"Mr. Hissle hates my playing."

"You told me he keeps asking you to demonstrate at quintet practice."

"Well, he changed his mind."

"Bastard. That doesn't make any sense."

If Dara quoted Mr. Hissle, Lily would tell her to quit. She would say Dara was lucky she had other talents, lucky she was getting a college degree. She would tell Dara to get the hell out of music.

Dara didn't want to hear it.

"Nice of Bella to leave us veal scaloppine," Victor said. He passed the silver tray of new potatoes down to Dara. "Buttered peas with almonds." Victor removed the lid from a casserole dish.

The chandelier was slightly dimmed, the heavy furniture lending an air of grandeur.

"Bernie Greenhouse called," Adele said. "The cellist in the Beaux Arts Trio," she added, turning to Dara. "Maybe you've heard of them?"

"Mother, please," Adam said.

"They want to have drinks after their concert next month. And, Victor, I forgot to mention Eugene Istomin. He'll be here next week for a fundraiser for Music from Marlboro. He can come to dinner Tuesday or Wednesday."

Dara was sinking. Istomin was a famous pianist, married to Pablo Casals's widow. Adele was talking about entertaining him as casually as if she were organizing a block party.

"Wednesday would be better," Victor said. "I have to teach late on Tuesday."

"You'll be home for dinner Wednesday, Adam, won't you?" Adele asked. "It would be nice for Eugene to see you."

Dara tried to fix her face to appear comfortable.

"Yeah, I'll be home," Adam said.

"Who else should we invite to dinner on Wednesday?"

"Can you come?" Adam said, turning to Dara.

"You're welcome to, dear," Adele said, as an afterthought. "Victor, what musicians should we invite?"

"Can I pass anyone the peas?" Victor asked, sliding the casserole dish toward the center of the table.

"I can't," Dara said. "Thank you," she added. "It's a school night."

"How are your lessons with Phillip going?" Adele asked. "Mr. Hissle, I mean."

"Fine." Dara plunged her fork into a potato. She felt as if she had subtitles across her forehead screaming out Mr. Hissle's tirade.

"Lucky he could take over for Isaac, don't you think?" Adele said.

Dara nodded and tried to smile. She looked at the wall in front of her, lined with scores, and scanned the bindings. There was so much music with which she was unfamiliar. Adele clearly considered her beneath them. Dara was wretched. It was only a matter of time before Adele got wind of Mr. Hissle's poor judgment of her.

Adam stood to clear the dishes. Dara followed, afraid to be left alone with Victor and Adele, who, despite Dara's reaction, were legendary hosts.

In the kitchen Adam wrapped his arms around her. "You look sad," he said.

"This is nothing like my house," Dara said.

"Your parents can think of something besides music."

"I don't know half of what you guys talk about."

"Like making dinner plans with Eugene Istomin?"

"I can't fit in," she said softly.

"Dara!"

"Other girls would know a lot more about music."

"Who cares?" He brushed back the hair on Dara's forehead and leaned over to kiss her.

"It's hard without Isaac, isn't it?" he said.

The following week, Dara trudged upstairs to her lesson. "Mr. Hissle?" She took out her viola. "Would you mind if I warm up for a minute before we get started on the Hindemith?"

"I would have thought you'd do that before your lesson." He settled into his folding chair.

"I came straight from Penn."

Hearing no response, Dara faced the door, pulling her bow across the strings in long tones. Some days, it was only five or ten bow strokes before she got blood running to her fingers and found her sound. But there was no magic today; she couldn't access the deep place where her best tone came from. Her fingers were cold and stiff. Concerned that Mr. Hissle was losing patience, she gave up. "I guess you want to hear the Hindemith?" she asked, opening her backpack to take out the music.

"Is that what you have for me today?"

Had he forgotten already? "You asked me to prepare it," she said. She'd spent the last week locked in her dorm room practicing, and she'd requested extensions on two papers to learn the damn thing.

She set the music on the stand and started in. The dissonances were more pronounced than they should be. She sounded like a bad orchestra tuning up. Her fingers were frozen. Mistake after mistake flew by. When she finished, she put her instrument down and said, "Maybe I could try it again?"

"Did you practice that?" Mr. Hissle shook his head from side to side, speaking through pursed lips. "No ears, no ears at all. I don't know why Koroff bothered."

She bit her lip hard. She refused to cry in front of Mr. Hissle.

"I'll hear it again next week, but I don't see any reason for you to take up my time today," Mr. Hissle said. He was out the door before she'd closed her case.

Isaac must have been too soft on her. Dara couldn't hold on to Isaac's voice, or Mrs. Koroff's parting words, "Isaac thought the world of you." Isaac, who had students playing in the best orchestras, who must have been able to judge who was musically worthy. Mr. Hissle had expunged him from memory. Isaac's fat, generous sound had disappeared, and Dara didn't know where to find it.

Dara closed her case and started down the steps. At the foot of the stairs, Mr. Hissle and Adele Pearl were chatting. Adele looked up. "Hello, Dara. How are you? I know you two are acquainted," Adele said cheerily, gesturing to Mr. Hissle.

"Just finished a lesson," Mr. Hissle said.

Dara looked from Mr. Hissle to Adele and back again. "Have to go," she said, hurrying out the door.

When Adele heard what Mr. Hissle had to say, she wouldn't want Dara spending time with her son. If Dara left Adam now, she could preempt his breaking up with her. He would find a girlfriend in his league. He would like that better.

22

"Adam," Dara said. In the fluorescent light of the coffee shop, she stirred her cup idly. It was a humid April day. She was unusually pale. "You need to be with a real musician."

Adam knew she was upset—her voice was flat—but he didn't know why. "What are you talking about?"

"I'm not the right girlfriend for you. You need a musician." She was hardly audible.

Adam leaned across the table, raising his voice. "Dara! Look at me." He reached for her hand, but she put it in her lap.

"I have to leave." She was starting to choke up.

"Dara!" He felt like screaming.

"It would be better if you forgot about me."

"Dara," he said, "I'm trying to say something."

She raised her hand in protest. "I can't listen to any arguments. It's the right thing."

She stood up and hurried out, as if turning back would cause a cataclysm.

What was she talking about? Better off without her? What kind of twisted logic was that? Adam nearly mowed down a waitress as he rushed to the door to catch her. But Dara was out of sight.

Back at his seat, confounded and crushed, Adam opened the packets of sugar stacked in the plastic holder at the end of the table. He shook them one by one into his coffee cup, took the little creamers and emptied them into Dara's cup, then poured one cup into another, back and forth, mixing a muddy gray brew into each saucer.

What was wrong with her? She seemed possessed. Upset and frightened, Adam didn't know how he could have been clearer, or more reassuring. She had shut down.

Adam walked into the muggy, wet Philadelphia afternoon. It started to pour. He couldn't see a block ahead but there was no reason to hurry; he was already soaked.

Would she pay attention if he wrote to her? Went to her dorm? Cried in the middle of Rittenhouse Square? He would try—nobody would try harder—but he was miserable with the certainty that no matter how contorted Dara's logic, she would not yield. Hadn't she run off in fury when she found out he'd known Isaac was sick? This was bigger than that.

Adam arrived home to the booming sounds of his parents' practicing. Ambling into the living room, he stood dripping—hot and chilled—as his father looked up from his score. Victor motioned Adele to stop.

"Adam, take off your wet things! Please don't flood the living room." Adele picked up a pencil to mark something on her score.

"Dara's left me," Adam said.

"What happened?" Adele asked.

Victor got up from his piano bench and put his arms around his devastated, wet son. "Come dry off and we'll talk."

Adam shook his head. "There's nothing to say." He wiped a hand across the water trickling down his forehead. "She just announced she was leaving. I don't know why. But I can tell she means it."

"I know it's hard," Adele said. "But there are always other girls out there... She seems to lack the requisite commitment."

"Well, then," Adam said in a quiet, burning fury, "you must be relieved."

Adele's face fell. "Adam, how can you say that?"

"Your mother loves you," Victor said hurriedly. "We both do. Such a nice girl. Maybe it would help to read something." Victor got up to fetch the record jacket to Pearl and Pearl playing Rachmaninoff. "Listen to this. It's a beautiful poem called 'Tears.'"

"Victor!" Adele exclaimed. "You can't take away someone else's pain with words. All you can do is give them music."

"Music!" Adam laughed cynically. "That's what did us in. At least Dara thinks so."

"Who knows what's going on with her?" Victor asked. "There may be things you're not aware of."

"Like the fact that my mother thinks my girlfriend 'doesn't have the requisite commitment'? Gee, I wonder if Dara ever picked up on that? I bet she thinks all I care about is my violin. Screw the violin! You two can go back to your practicing."

&

"If you're this upset, you have to apologize to him," Victor said, clicking off the bedroom light.

"I am upset, but it's disingenuous to apologize," Adele said. "He'll see through it."

"Jesus, Adele. Who cares about being right? Isn't being his mother more important? Can you at least talk to him?" Victor wanted to shake her.

"Does he think I'm that much of an ogre?"

"Don't blow it out of proportion." Victor slid under the covers. "Kids don't see things from their parents' perspective. It would help if you reached out."

"He's not a kid, and besides, we're such a close family," Adele said. "We've tried so hard. After your mother skipped our wedding, we promised ourselves we'd never be alienated from our child."

"Well, don't start now," Victor said. "He's choked up about a girl, and he's a sensitive young man to begin with. He's crazy about Dara."

"I don't see why."

"It has nothing to do with you. You're not him. We made our romantic choices; he gets to make his. Whether she's got talent isn't relevant. Besides, she's clearly got enough brains to go around."

Adele rested her head on Victor's chest. "Don't you think Adam would be better off with a musician?"

"Oh for heaven's sake! Who said he's getting married? He fell in love for the first time."

"It would be easier for him to be with a musician. It was for us."

"He's not us. Why can't you remember that?"

"I'll try."

"Are you going to talk to him?"

"I'll sleep on it. I'm afraid to make it worse," Adele said.

"No," Victor said, "you're just plain afraid."

23

Dear Dara,

I'm writing one last time, even though I haven't heard from you. I'm leaving to study at the Paris Conservatory for a year. My parents are making me go because they're terrified I'll never practice again. What a disaster that would be!

More than you know, I hope you're well.

Love, Adam

Adam not practicing? It was like the sun not rising in the east. Dara couldn't stand to think about it. She needed to hold on to her tenuous conviction that she'd done the right thing. But no matter how hard she tried to suppress it, Adam's last, agonized look was branded in her memory.

PART III

Longing is at the very source of existence, insofar as people are born of love.

—Josef Škvorecký, *The Bass Saxophone*

24

Dara scrolled through emails in her office at Penn, pretending to work. Fortunately, none of her students had shown up for office hours.

Would it be a bad idea to go to one of Adam's concerts? The news of Adele's death made Dara long to hear him play. She could sit on the aisle and dash out before the lights came up. He wouldn't have to know she was there.

On the other hand, she'd had twenty years to attend one of his concerts and hadn't done so.

What if he didn't remember her?

She checked the New Philadelphia Trio's schedule. Their next concert was on the night she taught a seminar. She exhaled in relief. And felt slightly let down.

Maybe she would try to get to Adele's memorial concert.

25

Adam signaled the final cadence of the New Philadelphia Trio's performance. He couldn't see the audience through the glare of the stage lights, but he could hear their enthusiasm. Together with Patti and Thaddeus, he stood to acknowledge the applause.

He looked back at Patti shimmering in a magenta gown, one hand on the piano. Her hair was pinned up in a sparkly barrette, her cheeks flushed with pleasure.

Adam pulled his violin diagonally across his chest and bowed once more, then slowly raised his head, mentally imploring Dara. *Are you out there? Come to the stage door. Please.* Hadn't she promised?

"When is your coach going to let your trio perform?" Dara had asked one afternoon long ago, hunched over a book on his bed.

He put down his violin. "Maybe in the spring."

"Tell him to let you guys play; I want to hear you." She'd turned the page and returned to her reading.

He'd bent down and kissed the top of her head, taking in the fruity smell of her shampoo, then resumed practicing.

"I'll come to every concert you ever give," she'd said.

Adam hadn't questioned the absurdity of her resolve. Where was she now? She may as well have been a fleeting butterfly. She'd kept a commitment, but it had been her commitment to leave him.

During his student days in Paris, Adam's landlady, Madame Cliquot, woke him every day. "*Bonjour!* You can't sleep through your classes at the *Conservatoire.*" The mornings were cold and dark. "I have a *café* for you; then you have to go."

He sensed Madame's perfume before he opened his eyes. She was in her early forties, her hair parted down the middle, a blond bun resting above her neck. Adam felt the imprint of her whisper as he crawled out of bed, careful to avoid hitting his head on the sloping ceiling.

He splashed water on his face and made his way down the narrow steps to her kitchen. Madame wore a calf-length blue work jacket as she went about her chores: cleaning her boarders' rooms, preparing their meals, and scrubbing the kitchen floor. There was a Monsieur Cliquot, but he traveled, leaving early in the morning with a briefcase and train ticket in hand.

"You would never get to school if I didn't throw you out of bed." Madame smiled and handed him a bowl of steaming *café crème*.

Adam dreaded heading to class. In his ensembles he played halfheartedly. He couldn't pick up the linguistic nuances of Pascale and Nicole's exchanges as they giggled their way through trio rehearsals. When their conversation accelerated, Adam was sure they were teasing him. It made him feel old. And isolated.

What had he done to make Dara leave him? Why had she been so sudden and definite? He couldn't find the concentration to practice.

"Such a sad face," Madame Cliquot said, sliding the jam pot and a basket of brioche toward him.

"Just tired," Adam said.

She looked up from rinsing the coffee pot. "No, I think you are sick with love. Will she return?"

Adam shook his head.

"*Le pauvre,*" she said. "There will be others."

Whenever possible, Adam left his violin in his room and walked Paris. He took in patisserie displays—buttery croissants, glistening fruit tarts, little round chocolate cakes lined up like rows of a chorus. The smell of fresh bread as women emerged from boulangeries with baguettes hanging from their straw baskets.

Fromagerie windows, with creamy rings of cheese dusted in light ash, or enveloped in rind.

Adam listened to the city. Merchants sloshed water along the curb toward the gutter. Leaves from plane trees crunched underfoot. Diminutive cars, horns bleeping, sped over boulevards. Adam learned the prolonged high pitch of the *Métro*'s closing doors, followed by a whoosh of rubber wheels.

Elegantly composed buildings framed a visual tableau. The tricolor waved triumphantly over ornate palaces dispensing justice. Notre Dame—majestic, assured—lit the night.

Adam spent whole days at the Louvre, sitting in empty galleries searching the eyes of Madonnas or watching clouds drift over Dutch landscapes. A wing of the museum celebrated ancient Egypt; there were rooms of amphorae with lusty Greeks painted around the rims.

Daylight was scarce. In the heart of winter, the sun rose after eight thirty and set by four. The air was damp. Fog shrouded the Eiffel Tower. Adam wandered down to the river, water swishing against its banks. He sat on a bench and looked at the bridges punctuating the meandering Seine, and rehearsed forgetting.

His parents visited in early January before traveling to a performance in Lyon.

"Are you practicing?" his mother asked over escargots at a corner bistro.

"Adele, please!"

"Not much," Adam said.

"Adam, you can't let yourself go. You know you can't."

"You're right, I do know. I don't need reminding. I'm getting acquainted with Paris. Isn't that why you sent me here?"

He got scared when the conductor at the Paris Conservatory moved him to the back of the first violin section. He couldn't deny how sloppy his orchestra playing had become. He was fulfilling the stereotype of the complacent violinist, last in the section. "Deadwood" was the musicians' term. His fingers had never been so stiff. He slid around the strings, his precision gone.

One Saturday morning it was raining too hard to go out. Adam stared out the gauzy curtains of his bedroom to the sidewalk below. A few people hurried under umbrellas. Not a single car or motorbike passed. He'd traveled all the way to Paris, and it looked as uninviting as Philadelphia in November.

He was alarmed at the state of his playing. Every day he was losing technique. The more time passed, the more daunting seemed the prospect of practicing again. He would return to the US a third-rate player.

There was a knock on his door. "Adam, I'm going out. Monsieur's mother is sick, and I have to get her medicine. Need anything?" Madame Cliquot had taken off her work coat. She was wearing a cobalt sweater dress. He could see the shape of her breasts and the curve of her hips. "It's not a day for errands, but *c'est la vie*."

Through the gauze curtains he watched her scurry down the sidewalk, purse clutched to her chest. He'd never seen her legs before.

Enough. No one was home to hear his rasping violin. He shut his bedroom door and wrestled his atrophied muscles. For six hours he played scales. Slowly, painfully, he progressed around the circle of fifths. His sound grated on him, but he persisted. Major scales, minor scales. Arpeggios. He felt like a malnourished child being given meat; it was hard to digest. He stopped frequently to shake out cramps in his hands. By the end of the day, he was exhausted.

On Sunday he started in again. This time, it took slightly less time to warm up. His bow felt more centered. He still couldn't contemplate playing music; he would stick to exercises until he could reclaim his tone.

What good was it to spurn his violin? He wasn't proving anything to his mother. He hated to admit she was right. "Letting himself go" made him miserable. Avoidance wouldn't bring Dara back. He could either continue to fight against all that was natural to him, or he could acknowledge that his violin was his most reliable companion.

His playing improved. He regained control of his hands and chose pieces for a recital at the end of the year. The giggling at trio rehearsals diminished.

He was in a deep sleep when he heard the latch to his door open. Madame Cliquot tiptoed into his room. She touched her index finger to her lips and slipped under the covers. Her blond hair spilled over her shoulders. Adam had never seen it down before.

He reached under her satin nightdress, pulled it over her, and pressed her body to him. The heat of a woman. The brush of her lips, her knowing fingers. Throwing off a long slumber, he slid his newly toned hands along her sides, clasped her rounded hips. She sank into him, her breasts bouncing in the shadows.

After she crept out, Adam watched the sun rise. Pink and purple streaked the Paris skyline. Downstairs, dressed in her blue work coat, Madame Cliquot handed him his *café crème* and wished him a good day.

After the trio concert, Adam wrapped his violin in its blue silk bag and unscrewed the end of his bow, gathering his things from backstage. Thaddeus called from behind the curtain, "Patti, you were magnificent. I'm afraid they're going to be disappointed when Vladimir comes back."

"Shall we go out to dinner to celebrate?" Adam asked.

"I have to get home," Thaddeus said. "I haven't seen my boy in too long. He'll be asleep, but at least I can peek in on him."

Adam felt a tinge of envy for the family that anchored Thaddeus, family that Thaddeus created. Adam had watched Thaddeus and Francesca get together. She and Thaddeus worked as servers in the same restaurant when Thaddeus was going through Caldwell. They'd been together forever. Francesca was now in social work school. They were crazy about their boy.

Patti joined Adam. "I'll come," she said, smiling.

"Great!" Adam said with affected cheer. He was disappointed that Thaddeus wouldn't join them. What would he and Patti talk about? They would rehash the concert. Perhaps that would take a whole dinner. They would end up at Patti's apartment. Frankly, he wouldn't mind missing dinner and going straight to her place.

How much longer could he keep up this charade? Adam didn't like Patti harboring expectations he couldn't fulfill. He was ashamed that he hadn't leveled with her. For all their time spent together, they were virtual strangers. Why couldn't he take responsibility and end it?

Meanwhile, time was running counterclockwise. Maybe among her powers, Adele Pearl had caused its inversion. Before his mother's death, Adam had conceived of himself as living an ordered existence; he practiced, his trio performed a dozen concerts each year, he taught his students. He understood his place within the family constellation as gifted son of the renowned Pearl and Pearl team. Not as well-known perhaps, but a respected musician in his own right.

He disliked his nagging fixation with his mother and Hissle. He was irritated every time he thought about them, which was too often. His negativity was distracting. He didn't want his mood controlled by his mother, whether she was alive or dead.

On the other hand, Adam delighted in Victor's progress—measure by measure, note by note. Too, Adam's daily walks through Philadelphia's streets to the Schuylkill River had become indispensable. Those rowers in their sculling boats, steadily pulling their oars, seemed to know something Adam needed to learn.

"Shelby's for steak?" Patti asked.

"Sounds good," Adam said. He picked up his violin case and followed her out the stage door.

26

I've made a decision," Victor said, closing the keyboard in his studio at Caldwell. "I've accepted a two-week residency at Aspen."

Adam sat in the chair next to the piano. "Dad, that's fantastic."

"'Decide' isn't quite the right word. But I told them I'd come. It'll be a long plane ride to Denver without Adele. She would get excited planning dinner dates with musicians from overseas. In that short hop from Denver to Aspen, the plane flies low. The scenery is gorgeous. Snowy mountaintops. Sunshine. It was ours for the summer."

"It'll do you good, Dad."

"I've never been the planner," Victor went on. "That was your mother. She got us into the world and figured out how to promote us."

"Organized your tour schedules."

"Followed everyone else's too," Victor said. "Invited them over when they were in town. Reached out to their kids when they started at Caldwell."

"Can I ask about Hissle?" Adam asked, concerned about being too overt.

"There's nothing you can't ask me."

"Did Mother keep close tabs on him?"

"Mother?" He laughed. "No more than anybody else. She did help him get a full-time job replacing Isaac Koroff. She felt bad he'd been fired from the Karminsky Quartet."

"Fired?"

"He's not the easiest person to get along with."

"No kidding."

"It wasn't just his personality," Victor said. "The other members of the quartet thought his playing had gone downhill.

Your mother's theory was that Hissle was ignoring the group. Too much prima donna. Too loud, jumped the tempo. Things like that. She couldn't stand the scratch in his tone. He stuck out. The Karminsky normally blend well together."

"Why did she help him?"

"I didn't get involved. My job was to study the scores." Victor closed his eyes. "We were a way station for musicians coming through Philly. I wonder how your mother had the energy for it. Or how I did, for that matter. So many people, so much ambition. It could get frenetic. After the guests left, Adele would rehash everything, in case I'd missed something, although I usually hadn't. She needed me to listen to her."

"Keep her polished," Adam said.

Victor looked at Adam. "I heard her worries in the middle of the night."

"I never saw them," Adam said.

"No, I don't imagine you did. Neither did anyone else." Victor paused. "It's quiet now. A new life, different from before." He looked at Adam. "Can a man live two lives? How do people remarry? It sounds exhausting."

Adam heard the subtext. "What about getting married for the first time?"

Victor smiled. "What about it?"

"Haven't found the right person, I guess." Was that true? Maybe what Adam had seen growing up was unappealing. All work and no play. Or maybe a marriage like that of his parents was appealing, but Adam knew he'd never find that kind of professional kinship. "Sometimes I feel desperate to engage in anything but music," Adam said. "The beauty is easily sucked out. Too much drudgery and pettiness."

"I'm sure that's true in any field," Victor said. "I bet astronomers discuss nothing but black holes, and firefighters nothing but arson."

Adam laughed. His personal and professional life revolved around the violin. Where was the variety? Maybe he was in an aesthetic stupor.

"The things you learn!" Victor said. "Death is all around. But when it's your wife, your musical better half, you're the first to experience it." He stood up from his piano bench. "I guess we each grieve in our own way. Time to head home." He was gone before Adam could ask him about the memorial concert. Or follow up on Hissle.

Adam headed to his studio. *Dad, can't you see it? Hissle and Mother?*

Why couldn't Adam shut this down? Victor didn't need Adam's assistance. He was certain of himself and of his love, qualities Adam not only admired but coveted.

Adam opened the door to his studio and set his violin case on a chair. The questions Adele left behind! Adam couldn't grasp the finality of her death. As he removed his violin from its blue satin bag, he realized he was lucky to have spent time with her at the end, to have experienced the serenity of sitting with her body. To have held her hands and said goodbye in his own way. Adele had shown Adam that he didn't need to hide from death. Really, her bravery was awe-inspiring. Adam felt deepened and stretched even as he was befogged by mysteries. He preferred this place of wonder to fixating on an unpleasant viola teacher with scratch in his tone.

He had a vision of Hissle opening his studio door and glaring at him after Dara had completed her chamber music coaching session.

I wasn't waiting for you, Phillip Hissle. I was waiting for Dara.

27

Something simple," Patti said, dishing out seared beef and onions from the frying pan. Her apartment smelled of soy sauce and ginger. She was efficient over her narrow stove, maneuvering in a tight space. "We have rice too," she said, scooping from a rice cooker that took up most of the counter. She handed Adam his plate. She was wearing a white apron tied around a beige cashmere sweater. "I think we're set." She sat down and smoothed the apron over her skirt.

Adam's knee bumped the underside of the table as he uncrossed his legs and stretched them out.

"See what I mean? My place is too small for you," Patti said, smiling.

He moved his feet to the left of her chair. "Thanks for dinner. It's delicious."

"And your place is too small for my piano," she said, glancing at the baby grand that filled the room. Patti was speaking with the same detached delivery as a few weeks before. "Spring is supposed to be a good time to move," she added.

Adam couldn't afford an apartment bigger than his. Patti probably earned less than he did. Maybe her family had money. Oh hell, why didn't he just say it? He didn't want to think about money around Patti. It felt too domestic and real. "Patti," he said, "I'm not going to be able to. I can't move in with you."

She put down her fork and waited for him to continue. "I can't make a commitment to you," he said. He sounded like a beginning music student, banging and scratching with no idea where he was going. She was silent, her expression blank.

"There's no one else," Adam said, stupidly raising the possibility. "I feel bad."

Her expression wasn't blank exactly; Adam just didn't know how to read it.

Patti quieted her body—no blinking or breathing or movement whatsoever. She trained her attention on Adam and watched him flail. He was deluded if he expected to be rescued. "It's not fair to you," Adam said, grasping for an appropriate phrase.

Patti looked puzzled, as if she were trying to formulate the right words. Adam heard Adele. *What are you doing, casting off a lovely young woman with talent and drive?* "I'm going through a lot right now," Adam added, like an awkward teenager.

"I know how you feel about your mother, Adam," Patti said. "I feel the same way."

No, Patti did not know how he felt. Even he didn't know how he felt.

"Such a great loss," Patti said. "Adele was my mentor. She leaves a huge hole. I cry whenever I think about her."

If this was Patti trying to console him, she was only making him miserable.

"One thing I admired about your mother was her forthrightness," Patti said. "She never left you guessing. You knew what she thought." She scrutinized Adam. "She wanted the best for you."

Adam squirmed. How could Patti know that? Adele had been a poor judge of what was best for him. Had Patti and Adele discussed him?

"More?" Patti motioned to the food on the table.

"No, thanks," Adam said, glancing at his plate. "I'm still working on this." He was making a mess of things; he was no different from any other man, commitment-averse and avoidant. The type women complained about.

"Your father invited me to play at Adele's memorial concert," Patti said.

Adam was stunned. Victor was making plans without him?

"He's excited about my contract with Deutsche Grammophon for the French Suites," she said. "He said I should choose one for the concert."

Why had it never occurred to Adam that Patti talked to his

father? They were colleagues; their studios were down the hall from each other. Did Adam really think he was the only one Patti talked to? He was appalled with himself. And he understood, not for the first time, that Patti was ambitious—why not, with her talents?—and that Victor might be a means to further her career, and again, why not? It was necessary to create a network of musicians who could help you professionally. Patti was doing what was expected, indeed, highly recommended. Adele would have been proud.

"Well," Patti said, measured and composed, "I guess we're done." She brought the dishes over to the sink.

It dawned on Adam that he was breaking up with Patti. More accurately, she was breaking up with him. He hadn't anticipated how smoothly she had taken control of the conversation, nor how firmly she'd ensured its finality. He felt checkmated and, in a far corner of his mind, impressed. He'd underestimated her.

He stood to go.

Patti's dignity was stinging. She wasn't going to give him the satisfaction of arguing. She wouldn't defend herself, because she didn't need defending. She wasn't going to cry, because she had too much self-respect.

"Everything was delicious," Adam said. "Thank you."

Adam started down Delancey Street toward home. He was in shirtsleeves, and it was windy.

His conversation with Patti felt one-sided, as if he'd played a duet part alone. By snuffing out whatever he and Patti had together, he'd amplified his grief. He thought grief was supposed to be unalloyed sadness, but his was a jumble of contradictory emotions. Remorse was part of it. A larger part was vacancy.

Chastened by Patti's mettle, he hugged his chest for warmth. Maybe, at last, he was finished with his series of unsatisfying liaisons. They were not relationships. They were dalliances, no matter how long they'd lasted. He was disappointed in himself. He walked slowly, afraid to go home for fear of being left alone with his thoughts.

As he neared Rittenhouse Square, his disappointment gave way to anger. Adele had neglected to see him for who he was. Her own son! She'd intended for him to fulfill her ambitions, making it inevitable that he'd let her down. She hadn't considered what Adam might want or what was best for him.

What was best for him?

Yesterday he'd been moved by his mother's bravery. Tonight, he felt unhinged. Why was he blaming Adele? She was dead; she would be dead forever. Adam could do as he pleased. He'd had this agency for years; he'd simply failed to exercise it. He'd been adept at identifying what he didn't want, uncertain of what he did.

No wonder he was stunned that Patti and Victor had discussed Adele's memorial. He'd clung to his concept of Patti, disembodied from her past, as if she'd been born when she arrived in Philadelphia to study with Adele. Was Adam any different from his mother, trying to shape Patti into his own creation?

Thaddeus once told Adam that when he became a father, he declared a statute of limitations on complaints about parents. Thaddeus must be right. Adam was in his late thirties, too old for these mental ravings. He'd rather follow Victor's example, acting the old pro, inching forward, figuring out his needs.

Adam opened the door to his apartment. No need for lights; it was bright enough at this hour, close to ten p.m. Cars streamed by below, police sirens wailed. Tall buildings lit up the city as far as he could see. He sat on his bed and sighed. All the contradictions: the sadness, the anger, the sense that his mother had become unknown to him. He was neither father nor husband. He wasn't even a boyfriend anymore. Unlike his parents, he had no dependents. Pearl and Pearl had been dependent on each other, two tributaries flowing into a river. Was there such a thing as half a river?

For the first time since his mother's death, Adam put his head in his hands and sobbed. Was there such a thing as a duet for one?

28

Built-in shelving! In Manhattan this place would have cost your firstborn with interest," Lily said, as she surveyed the piles of books on Dara's living room floor. "A Saudi sheik couldn't afford this."

Dara laughed. "I don't think Saudi sheiks settle in West Philly."

Dara showed Lily the kitchen.

"Okay, maybe a sheik wouldn't go for the slope in the linoleum floor," Lily said. "And cabinets that stick. But damn! Two stories, a bedroom upstairs? That's excellent."

"I feel great about the whole thing," Dara said, waving her arm around. "My own digs. I love coming home. I love the fact that I've made it a home. Our old place had no personality. You never saw it, did you?"

"You mean the 'marital abode'?"

Dara grimaced. "So-called. Tea? Beer? Wine?"

"Beer would be great, but you probably only have imported crap, right?"

"Right," Dara said.

"Make it tea."

Dara filled the kettle. "Matthew's place was a study in modernism. Couldn't have been more of a contrast to this. Antiseptic. Can you imagine keeping every surface clean, living with no clutter?"

"Nope," Lily said.

Dara thought of the dinner party a few years after she'd started teaching at Penn, where mutual friends introduced her to Matthew Johnson. There were a dozen people at an informal gathering over chili, baskets of tacos and bowls of shredded lettuce and cheese lining the center of a long table. She knew most everyone but hardly had a chance to socialize before Matthew sat next to her and began monopolizing her.

He'd come from work. He removed his tie and jacket and rolled his pink shirtsleeves to his elbow. His forearms were covered in blond hair. He wrapped his arm around the back of her chair and fixed his gaze.

"Tell me what you do."

"The same as most people here, teach at Penn." Her face got warm.

"You can do better than that! What subject?"

She laughed. "English."

"If I were a colleague, you'd never answer that way. Let me try again. What's your subject?"

"Victorian literature."

"That's a start. Tell me about your courses this semester. Then I want to hear about what you're publishing next."

She could tell he was an athlete; he was fit and windburned. After going on too long about the article she was researching, she stopped abruptly. "I have no idea what you do."

"Guess."

"Center City lawyer. Partner at one of those firms whose name sounds like the *Mayflower* manifest."

"Our host tipped you off."

"It's written all over you. Law school at Harvard or University of Virginia?"

"Very good! Harvard."

"Are you a runner?" She tilted her head. "Skier? No, maybe it's sailing."

"Two points again! Marathons. Do you answer your office phone, or does someone pick it up for you?"

"We have an administrative assistant for the department, if that's what you mean."

"Would she put me through to you?"

"Depends how courteous you are."

He called the next day. On Saturday night they ate at a fish restaurant on Twentieth Street. It was quiet, with blue-tinted lights, the kind with waiters who knew when and how to clear dishes without interrupting conversation.

"Nightcap at my place?" he said, helping her on with her coat and opening the door for her.

"I don't do this, you know."

"Do what?"

"Go to strange men's apartments after dinner."

"I'm not a strange man; I'm your very respectable date." He pulled her toward him in the middle of the sidewalk and kissed her, his tongue in her mouth before she could think about it.

"Maybe just this once," she whispered.

So this is seduction, she thought lazily as one a.m. swam by and she lay spent in his bed, her half-empty glass of cognac on the nightstand. His apartment had the latest in sound equipment, with lighting and understated black furniture that suggested the hand of a savvy decorator.

"How did I marry such a cliché?" Dara asked Lily.

"You never got your sorry ass out of the library in grad school," Lily said.

Dara laughed.

"At least you're laughing," Lily said. "I've never seen you such a mess as when that lame excuse for a man shacked up with his secretary."

Mornings, Dara would watch Matthew dress for work. He had a specific way of crimping his tie. With his Italian leather briefcase, he looked terribly responsible.

Their marriage felt inevitable.

"Lils, I'm getting better. I swear I am."

"Really?"

"C'mon! I got tenure, and I left Matthew. Still pinching myself about the tenure part."

"You goddamn should be pinching yourself, a smarty-pants like you. Do you have any sugar?"

"Just honey."

"Figures."

"As far as Matthew is concerned, there are no complications to argue about. My lawyer says he'll settle at the eleventh hour to avoid damning evidence coming out in public."

"You mean screwing his secretary? Is that even scandalous these days?"

"Apparently. Let's hope my lawyer is right." Dara stood and turned off the slow drip coming from the tap. "Don't know what I would have done without you, Lils."

"You would have spent more time torturing yourself. Speaking of torture, what about my goddamn ballet classes? I play the same pieces week after week for a bunch of anorexic girls with teachers who never want anything beyond Chopin. For this I went to Juilliard?"

"Sucks. Are you playing any chamber music?"

"Some. We applied for a grant to commission a new piece for piano, horn, and violin with accompaniment by African drum."

"Brahms, redux?"

"Not this guy. He's from Ghana. He's into cross-cultural up the wazoo. World music kind of thing."

"Sounds cool! When do you hear about the grant?"

"Maybe by the end of the year, which, come to think of it, is soon. Fortunately, I have plenty of holiday jobs. Every investment firm and their brother needs some class at their annual Christmas party. That's me, classy!" Lily said, standing up. "Girl, I'm starving. Let's go find food."

29

I asked Patti Lee to play a French Suite at Mother's memorial," Victor said, stretching his legs in his green easy chair. "I heard," Adam said. He didn't want to discuss Patti with his father.

"You did?" Victor sounded mildly surprised. "And I'll want Chopin. I think Patti's up to it, don't you?"

"Sure," Adam said, certain he couldn't have done worse in that last conversation with her. How was his trio going to get through their commitments before Vladimir finished rehab?

"You and I have to play the Franck," Victor said.

"I don't think I've ever played with you, Dad." It wasn't only this iconic piece; Adam had never played with his father at all. Once more, Adam was blanketed in his mother's missing-ness. Adam could do nothing to make his parents' duet whole; no one could. Not for the first time, Adam wondered how his father would get through this concert.

"I don't know why we haven't played together, son," Victor said, misty-eyed. "You played with your mother plenty of times growing up. Remember the drama around *Vocalise*? I don't know who that wretched boy was who bullied you, but your mother should have dealt with him right away."

"Water under the bridge," Adam said.

"I was so furious I couldn't see straight," Victor said. "Why didn't Adele just call the damn school?"

"I guess she thought that was your job," Adam said, realizing with renewed clarity that his father had filled many stereotypical "mother" roles. Adam's school friends' fathers never took them to the doctor or to buy new shoes. Their fathers never did any of the myriad things Victor had done with Adam. "I was lucky," Adam said, warmed by a burst of happy memories. Adam loved those little excursions, part man-to-man, part father-son, Victor insisting that they stop at Rindelaub's Bakery on the north side of Rittenhouse Square for a sticky bun after their errands. "Don't tell Mother," Victor would joke. "She'll never let me near the piano with my sugary fingers."

"Mother's instincts were right," Adam said, replaying that long-ago scene of Bella rinsing off his face, Adele summoning him to the living room with his violin, and his parents' bitter argument afterward. "I did feel better playing *Vocalise*. It was gorgeous."

"I'll have to settle for that," Victor said.

"How about...?" They spoke at the same time.

"I agree," Victor said, smiling. "We'll play *Vocalise* in homage to life in the Pearl family."

What was life in the Pearl family? The empty spaces that marked Adele's absences were as consequential as the pillars she built. Had that been her intention? To force independence on her son, to hurry him into adulthood? Adam had been an eager participant, joining his parents' soirées, teaching alongside them on the Caldwell faculty. But since Adele's death, the whole picture was in doubt, with Adam wondering if he was stuck in arrested development, still aching for his mother's approval—which would never come—while wearing the trappings of adulthood.

"One more request, Dad," Adam said, "the andante movement to the *Brahms Piano Quartet Opus 60*. I'll get our trio to do it. I just need to find a violist." He would invoke Dara, the two of them making love in his childhood bedroom. He didn't care that no one would get the allusion. He would do it for himself.

"Fine," said Victor.

30

Adam walked down the aisle toward the small stage at Caldwell for rehearsal. Victor was checking the height of the piano bench, hands rolling the side knobs. He wore a navy-blue blazer, white oxford shirt with a green paisley tie, and pressed gray flannel pants.

"Dashing, as always," Adam said, opening his violin case. His father never stepped out in casual clothes.

"We aim to please," Victor said wryly.

Adam set his music on the stand and tuned to Victor's A. As Victor sank into the opening of the Franck Sonata, Adam readied an up-bow to join the piano. Separate from the story of his parents' first meeting, Adam loved this sonata, with its butterscotch chords and lush melodies. He wouldn't have encouraged Alice Chang to program it for her recital otherwise. The piece required intimacy as piano and violin exchanged fragments of melody and harmony in equal measure. The composer left room for elasticity in tempos—even elasticity within individual notes—stretching time itself.

Adam tilted his ear to his violin to ensure he shaped creamy, warm tones. It was effortless synchronizing with Victor, as if father and son were finishing a string of rehearsals rather than playing together for the first time. They didn't say much other than stopping to emphasize a dynamic marking or discuss a rallentando. Victor leaned back, arms extended, rousing harmonies from the keyboard. He sounded sublime—a confectioner pulling taffy—and looked sublime, as if there were no other purpose for his hands than to knead piano keys.

Adam saw that Victor was as attached to the piano as Adele had been, even if she had been more obvious about it. The Caldwell piano needed revoicing—perhaps a full restoration— but Victor evoked its best tone. He had played on grander and brighter pianos on stages around the world, but he was unfazed, master of his art, the piano the tool of his trade.

Viscous sonorities poured into the hall. Adam basked in contentment as delicious as it was rare. No wonder his parents had lived as they had. Who wouldn't want to play with Victor Pearl? Adele was spot-on; she'd invested in the right musician. Adam felt as his mother must have, cradled in Victor's reliability and world-class interpretive skills. Victor was no less demanding of himself than was any other virtuoso, but along with a full palette of musical colors, he communicated serenity. Victor knew what he had—he had worked hard for it—he just didn't flaunt it. He was foothold and inspiration both.

Adam's mother had had this with Victor, and for so long! She had lived her best life, had been fulfilled as a musician. Clever Adele, she'd figured it out early enough to make a career of it.

As Victor and Adam wrapped up their rehearsal with a run-through of *Vocalise*, Adam surrendered to bliss. Adele had been right; this frothy romance was soothing. Adam experienced the pleasure of teaming up with his father, who loved music as much as he loved his wife. And, Adam understood, as much as he loved his son.

31

ADELE HAMMOND PEARL MEMORIAL CONCERT
Independence Theatre
February 6, 2005

Two o'clock p.m.

Hosted by Victor and Adam Pearl
Joined by Faculty from the Caldwell Institute of Music

French Suite No. 1 in D Minor, BWV 812 Johann Sebastian Bach

> *Allemande*
> *Courante*
> *Sarabande*
> *Menuet I*
> *Menuet II*
> *Gigue*

Nocturnes   Frédéric Chopin

> *B-flat Minor, op. 9, no. 1*
> *E-flat Major, op. 9, no. 2*
> *B Major, op. 9, no. 3*

Piano Quartet in C Minor, op. 60   Johannes Brahms

> *Andante*

Pause

Vocalise   Sergei Rachmaninoff

Sonata in A Major   César Franck

> *Allegretto ben moderato*
> *Allegro*
> *Recitativo-Fantasia: Ben moderato–Molto lento*
> *Allegretto poco mosso*

Dara sat in the mezzanine, coat around her shoulders. She was chilled from the blustery day and from entering a hall steeped in mourning. She scanned the stage, a grand piano slightly off-center, missing its twin like a poem shorn in half. She had come alone to dwell in the privacy of her memory, which contained a special wedge of time with Adam.

The hall lights dimmed; the crowd hushed. Patti Lee, dressed in black, made her way to the piano. She turned the knobs on the bench, then paused with her hands in her lap.

Staring at the glossy black piano, the raised lid poised for music, Dara felt as if she'd fallen through an hourglass timer. She closed her eyes. Music flowed, sacred and peaceful. Bach's first French Suite; the special tonality of D minor, a key signature that signaled sorrow.

She was a girl standing before the door to the Pearls' apartment, listening to Adele spin harmony, begging Adam not to go in. Anything to avoid disrupting Adele's flow. The memory was exquisite, and it was painful. She remembered Adam rubbing her back in the kitchen, enveloping her like a warm breeze, as if he understood the music's impact on her but wanted, too, to assert his independence from his mother.

Was that so? Dara hadn't appreciated his need for a separate identity from his parents. Dara's vision of the Pearls had been of a conjoined threesome that made judgments in unison. She saw now how unlikely that was. Really, it was absurd. That's not how families work. Children question their parents, and if they don't, they should.

Patti Lee's hands flew up and down in the second movement, soldiers marching in lockstep. Adele was known for her authoritative, forthright attack on the keyboard. Like Adele's, Lee's left hand drove the piece. And she could also embrace the keyboard, reluctantly parting with every note. The minuets were both serious and buoyant. The closing gigue brought heft.

Sound faded from the final bar, but no one dared break the

silence. Patti Lee turned to the audience and smiled but did not stand. Once again, she placed her hands in her lap.

Adam Pearl made his way onstage. Had he always been that tall? His hair was flecked with gray. He was wearing tails. It was a long time since Dara had seen him. He was graceful, poised. Lovely. He stepped to the microphone at the front of the stage.

"Good afternoon, ladies and gentlemen."

His voice ricocheted throughout the theater.

"My father and I are grateful for your attendance. No words of thanks could suffice for your generosity. This afternoon we celebrate the life of a wonderful musician. We remember my mother's great joy in performing. Without her, we cannot continue the Pearl and Pearl tradition of duo-piano music. Instead, the program is one she loved to teach and hear."

Dara ached. There was a reason why she had wanted him all those years ago.

"Join us after the concert for a reception in the lobby. We'll share our memories."

Was he married? Did he have children?

"Finally, my father and I want to extend special thanks to the musicians who have given their time, talents, and energy to make this celebration a reality."

He turned to acknowledge Patti Lee. She was at one with the piano, like Adele Pearl.

Victor sat quietly in the wings, the scores to *Vocalise* and the Franck Sonata resting in his lap, watching Patti melt into Chopin. Baleful melodies floated toward him. Adele had taught Patti well; Patti shared Adele's disciplined approach to playing and her intense focus.

Chopin had spanned Victor's musical lifetime, from his days at Juilliard to the present. From before Adele to after. But there would be no time after Adele. She was his other half, his foundation. She was as much a part of Victor's present as if she were living and breathing by his side. Not for the first time during these last months, Victor cherished the insight that

Adele inspirited him. That knowledge would have to carry him through today's performance.

Patti rose from her piano and walked backstage. Victor extended his hands. "You played beautifully, Patti. Adele would be proud."

❧

Dara was engulfed by Brahms. Adam, how could you? She had not paid attention to the program. Adam leaned into his instrument, weaving music from the early days of their relationship, the rich viola line singing Johannes Brahms's love note to Clara Schumann. Adam's gentle touch; he'd made her comfortable in her awkwardness. Pulling his bow across the strings, Adam angled first toward the cellist playing that haunting melody, then toward the pianist.

Adam.

Dara sighed and gazed around the audience. Across the mezzanine she saw Phillip Hissle, visible even in the dark of the concert hall. As if he'd felt her gaze, he looked from the stage toward her. It hadn't occurred to her that Hissle would be there. Why had she come? She had been hesitant and now saw her mistake. She trembled like a child facing punishment. Hissle was going to walk over and say something vicious. Not just about her viola playing, but about her marriage as well. *Once you were deaf, then you were blind.*

Adam and his father strode onstage. It was strange to see them as a pair. Dara recalled the foundational pair, Victor with his arm around Adele.

Victor and Adam started into *Vocalise*. Lush mellifluence; a song of sorrow.

Dara looked furtively toward Hissle. His black fedora was in his lap.

She turned back to the stage. Adam was playing by heart, looping melody through his father's accompaniment. He was born to play the violin. Lyricism, twinned with a commanding physical presence. Depth and maturity. His *Vocalise* was maple syrup pouring from a pitcher.

Adam and his father's playing was meshed and balanced in the Franck Sonata, Adam sensitive to the importance of the piano, and Victor careful to avoid overpowering his son.

Why had Dara been in such a hurry to leave Adam? She'd been infantile, her behavior more avoidant than anything else. It was cowardly not to have given him time to react. At least she'd grown up since then. She knew now that everyone experiences failure; there were always difficulties in finding a professional path. The best scholars stumbled. Dara was glad she'd studied music; it enriched her life.

Who ends up with their first love anyway? It isn't normal. You had to have other relationships, other experiences. She was grateful that Adam had been her first.

She shuddered to think about Lily's parade of horrors. If her first time—"a christening," as she'd put it—wasn't rape, it was perilously close. Lily was the strongest woman Dara knew. Lily had pushed on, had had a few boyfriends, none of whom deserved her. Last year Lily moved her parents across the country and took on the full burden of their care without losing her sense of humor. She performed whenever and wherever she could. Dara went to New York for her concerts. Other than the randomness of fate, it wasn't clear why Lily's career hadn't caught hold. Lily was still playing in venues that were too obscure for a musician with her gifts.

And then the concert was over. People clapped and stomped, smiling through tears. "What a pianist, what a teacher!" Dara caught scattered comments. "Adele was a guide and mentor, a friend to all." "What's Victor going to do?"

Dara pushed toward the exit, hoping to avoid Hissle. For heaven's sake, she was long past him.

Both sides of the mezzanine funneled down to the first floor. Dara had forgotten about the reception. Traffic was stopped in the lobby, jamming the stairwell. She looked down, wondering whether she would catch a glimpse of Adam. Had he been wearing a wedding ring? Violinists often don't; they can't have anything interfering with the free movement of their fingers.

Below, people were crammed in like groupies at a rock concert. Adam probably knew them all. Tables were spread with food. A bar was set up along one wall.

Dara was stuck in the center of the steps, unable to move. Hissle merged toward her, his fedora noticeable above the crowd. Jesus. He had seen her and was headed right for her.

She turned toward him. "Mr. Hissle." He stared ahead. She would conquer this. She tried again, speaking up. "Mr. Hissle." He seemed puzzled; his eyes were less piercing than she remembered.

"Dara Kingsley," she said, extending her hand. He looked down, trying to negotiate the next step.

He hadn't recognized her.

In the lobby, hundreds of people greeted each other, jockeying for positions near the refreshments. Hissle peeled off to the left.

Dara couldn't see the exit doors. She struggled to negotiate a path through the throng. She couldn't look for Adam; there were too many people. What would she say anyway? She maneuvered outside.

The air was frigid. She decided to walk home.

Dara was nothing to Hissle, not even a memory. He wasn't worth a cold second of her time. He couldn't do anything to her. So what if he was a two-bit sadist? Dara had seen her share of them in academia. They preyed on vulnerable young women. Abusive personalities extracted pleasure from attacking the right victim. She must have been one of a succession.

Dara strode west up Walnut Street, the wind blowing in her face. She felt a burden lifting, the closing of a chapter that mixed shame with a potent sense of failure. Hissle was nothing to her. He'd done nothing to waylay her career. She was where she wanted to be. Academically, at least.

What had she been grandstanding about, trying to persuade Adam that he needed to be with a better musician? She had been certain of her own rectitude, which she now saw as a mask for timidity. She'd fled from Adam in fealty to a bully. The thought made her recoil. No wonder she rarely replayed these events.

Which wasn't true. Dara did replay these events. Of course she did. She had been madly, passionately in love with Adam.

A wintry gust made her wish she'd worn a hat.

She'd convinced herself that she had been acting in Adam's best interests. That she was releasing him from his obligations to her, whatever those obligations meant at the time. If anyone had done that to her, Dara would have resented it. Imagine Matthew telling her to escape from him before it was too late. Dara had to make her own mistakes. Yet she'd tried to prevent Adam from making his.

What if Adele Pearl and Phillip Hissle had never even discussed Dara? Or what if they had, and Dara had projected Adele onto her son? Dara had been headstrong and narrow-minded. If there was one thing she tried to convey to her students, it was the necessity of examining problems from multiple angles. Discovering the richness of a text required deliberation.

Dara's feet were numb and her fingers frozen. Continuing west, she tightened her scarf and shoved her hands in her pockets. By the time she passed Thirtieth Street Station, she had surrendered to unfamiliar, consuming longing. Adam was a beautiful man, and she had run from him, two truths that rang louder than the closing bars of a Beethoven symphony.

Victor embraced his son as they stepped offstage. "It went okay, don't you think?"

"Good job, Dad. You did the right thing for Mother."

Adam felt relieved. He'd been fretting for weeks about whether Victor would make it through, whether there would be adequate seating, and whether he'd have the nerve to speak in public about his mother.

"Not done, are we?" Victor said.

"Too crowded," Adam said. "We'll never make it to the lobby if we go through the theater. Let's go around outside."

They walked out the stage door. As they turned the corner onto Walnut Street, Adam saw Dara. She was unmistakable, hurrying away from the theater, her chestnut braid swaying over a forest-green overcoat.

He was twenty-one again. *Dara! Did you recognize the Brahms? I programmed it for you like an acrostic in a poem. Dara, wait! I have things to ask. There are things I want to know.*

"Come in from the cold," Victor said, holding open the door.

"Thank you, Mr. Pearl." Patti came from behind and breezed past Adam.

Patti. She had performed magnificently. And had not said a word to Adam since that night, other than what was necessary during rehearsals.

"Time to face the multitudes," Victor said, winking. The front entrance to the theater was mobbed; there was hardly room to move.

Adam was assaulted by noise. Had he been crazy, leaving Patti?

There was no going back. Her silence made things clear.

People were pressing in on him, eager to console. A woman in a flamboyant turquoise caftan grabbed his arm. Adam couldn't remember her name. "I've lost the best friend I ever had. Nobody listened to my troubles the way your mother did."

Knowing it was futile, he craned his neck toward the door to see if Dara had changed her mind. He wondered where she had gone, and why she had come.

"Can I tell you a story about your mother?" a man in a tweed suit yelled across the table of crudités. Thaddeus shoved a glass of red wine toward Adam.

"Thanks," Adam said.

"What a class act your mother was." The concertmaster of

the Philadelphia Orchestra pumped Adam's hand. "We loved it when she and Victor played with us. Conductors ate out of her palm."

"Thank God for her recordings, Adam." An elderly cellist leaned on his cane. "It was hard enough making a go of a piano trio in those days, to say nothing of two pianos. Pretty nifty she managed it with your father. Where is the old boy?" He turned around and headed for Victor.

A man with a French accent said to Adam, "Mr. Pearl, I've never met you, but I studied with your mother at Caldwell when you were a baby. She kept pictures of you in her wallet."

"Really?"

"Of course! She was your mother."

Adam considered his mother's public face, much of it unrecognizable. The woman who opened her heart to everyone, the musical trendsetter. She worked harder than anyone he knew. But she wasn't being celebrated for her drive. It was astonishing the number of people who admired her not for her playing, but for her humanity.

Thaddeus pounded Adam on the back, his left arm wrapped around his cello case. "Bet you'll be glad to kiss this day goodbye."

"No kidding. You sounded great in the Brahms," Adam said. "Thanks, Thaddeus."

"Your parents were an amazing partnership," a short man with a gray mustache said to Adam. "I can't believe it's over." Adam smiled and nodded. So many things were over: Adam's family as he had known it; his hope that he would meet his mother on his terms rather than hers; the Pearl and Pearl duo-piano team, whom Adam had not fully accepted as over until he'd spoken into the microphone this afternoon at Independence Theatre.

Adam turned to check on his father. Victor was holding a plate of crackers and bobbing his head like a doll, pretending to hear above the din.

The crowd began to thin out.

Patti put her coat on and went over to Victor. "Adele would have been so pleased," he said to her. "Thank you."

Patti stood on tiptoe and kissed Victor's cheek. "I'd do anything for Adele," she said. She put on her gloves and left.

"There's Hissle," Victor said.

For the first time, Adam had a view to that side of the lobby. Hissle was standing at the bar, eating a plate of meatballs. Victor headed toward him.

"You could have asked me to play the Brahms," Hissle said as Victor approached.

"I chose the violist," Adam said, joining them. Hissle's eyes were rheumy and he was wearing hearing aids.

"It's time for the younger generation to have their day, don't you think?" Victor said lightly. He cocked his head toward Adam and said, "They're trustworthy." Victor turned back into the crowd that was milling around the bar.

"I wouldn't know," Hissle muttered.

Adam started to speak but refrained. Something was reorganizing itself, his vision coming into focus. What did it mean that this man, a musician, was losing his hearing? Hissle carried an air of diminishment and defeat. Adam was surprised to feel pity for him. Maybe that was why Hissle had been so nasty in the music library, why he had turned his headphones up to full volume—to avoid conversation.

"I met your mother at Tanglewood," Hissle said to Adam. "Adele wasn't acquainted with your father at that time. She met him later."

Adam thought back to his father's story, which he'd heard so often he had it memorized. While a student, Victor had gone to Tanglewood and fallen in love with Adele after hearing the Franck Sonata. He'd tried to congratulate her after the performance but couldn't get near. The next time they met, they were back at Tanglewood.

"And?" Adam said.

"I saw Victor," Hissle said. "I saw your father; with that height he's hard to miss. An overeager young pup trying to horn in on the pretty girl. No sense that she might have other interests." Hissle shook himself, as if he were emerging from a trance.

Adam tried to take that in. Victor horning in? Victor's version was a glowing appreciation of Adele's musicianship, a fan boy trying to get near a great musician. "She wouldn't give me the time of day after the concert," Victor had said.

"Afterward..." Hissle began.

"Afterward, what?"

"After she got together with your father, she treated me like she treated everyone else. She had a way of being friendly and cheerful that cut you off. I could never get underneath that. Makes you wonder."

"About what?"

Hissle stood and shuffled out, leaving a half-eaten plate.

"Hissle has no decorum, eh?" Victor said, returning to Adam.

"True," Adam said. What had Hissle meant? He wasn't so much menacing as pathetic, weakened by physical decay and isolated by a foul disposition, pining for something from Adele that he could never get.

"Hissle didn't have a family," Victor said. "He doesn't appreciate ours."

"I bet he's jealous," Adam said, considering this for the first time.

Adam thought of his family's standing in the musical firmament, their undeniable closeness. Looking through Hissle's eyes, Adam saw his family as a tight unit that shared a common language and common joy.

"Our family may be unconventional," Victor said, "but what a wonderful family we have."

"That must be it," Adam said. He looked at his father, who was weary but composed. The Pearl family worked in its own peculiar fashion, parents who raised a son while living their dreams, who treated Adam as one of them—the anointed— despite the holes in this approach.

"I wouldn't have had it any other way," Victor said, smiling.

"Mmm," Adam said, pleased to see Victor standing proud. Victor was weathering the loss of his spouse and career with equanimity. Adele had provided that. She left Victor a trove of love and support from beyond the grave.

No wonder Hissle was churlish. Now that Adam had tasted the satisfaction of playing with his father, it was obvious why Hissle resented Adele's desertion. Victor had earned Adele's trust, and Adele had returned it in spades. She launched and fostered their careers. She cemented a unique life partnership. Hissle had plenty to begrudge.

Victor scanned the lobby, now mostly empty. "I think we can call it a day."

"I'm glad it's over," Victor said, waving to the doorman at the entrance to his apartment building.

"Do you want me to come up, Dad?"

"No, you've done enough."

Adam kissed his father goodbye and, violin in hand, turned east to head home.

32

It was dark by the time Dara got home. She poured a glass of white wine and lay down on the sofa she'd found in a secondhand store on Pine Street. She loved that sofa, with its soft burgundy cushions and yellow tassels covering its stumpy legs.

She closed her eyes and replayed the afternoon's concert. The loss of Adele seemed to have deepened Adam's music-making. His violin was both limb and heartbeat.

The grace and elegance in his fingers, the same fingers that had traced her ankle bones and meandered up her legs, that had introduced her to her body, igniting a spectrum of sensations she hadn't known were hers. The brush of his bow on the strings, the brush of his palms on her skin. His long arms, his warm, naked body against hers. The silences between them that were the rests in the music.

Dara had once been an audience of one.

Where had the time gone? Dara hadn't spoken to Adam in nearly twenty years, hadn't seen him until today. Still, her past felt more sharply defined than her present—her wistful memory of peering into Adam's Briarly practice room, a single violinist creating enough sound to fill a concert hall.

It was true that Dara liked not answering to anyone. If she'd had a man in her life, or a child, her time wouldn't be her own. She understood the luxury of working into the small hours to finish a lecture or put final touches on a paper. She was relieved—and proud—to have completed the tenure marathon. On the other hand, she was treading water. She hadn't yet maintained a successful adult relationship and had done poorly at ending them. What kind of advice would Isaac offer? *Feel something, anything. Follow a clear vision, free of bitterness and regret.*

"Right!" Dara said to the books in her living room. She smiled, recalling Isaac's acerbic, self-deprecating humor and his drumbeat of encouragement. "Onward."

Adam walked toward his picture windows. Like Victor, Adam was relieved the concert was over. It had gone well, much better than he'd had a right to expect. He was pleased with his father's strength and self-possession.

Who was his mother? Would he ever understand her? Her public persona was different from the one Adam knew. It wasn't her open criticism. It was her habit of willfully ignoring what he might feel. No matter how many ways he turned it over, Adam couldn't understand this practice in any parent, let alone his mother.

He gazed out over the Delaware River and considered his mother's bequest to him: a lifetime to interpret the music. She nurtured his talent and oversaw an immersive musical education. He'd waited anxiously for her returns from Pearl and Pearl's tours, sought comfort under her soundboard, and later, served as her musical confidant.

Adam could think of more straightforward legacies. A set of fine china, perhaps, or a beloved piece of furniture. Or simple, unconditional love.

And Dara?

Adam had spotted her name on the list, and she had come. He was more focused on that reality than on the fact that she was married.

She was still running away.

33

ADELE PEARL MEMORIAL CONCERT
A FITTING TRIBUTE

Philadelphia. Along with hundreds of other appreciative listeners, the cream of the classical music establishment flocked to Independence Theatre yesterday afternoon to pay last respects to the eminent duo-pianist Adele Hammond Pearl, half of the Pearl and Pearl husband-and-wife team.

The program opened with a distinguished performance of Johann Sebastian Bach's first French Suite by Patti Lee, a former student of Adele Pearl, and now on the faculty at the Caldwell Institute of Music. Lee, who has secured a recording contract with Deutsche Grammophon for the complete set of French Suites, is a pianist worthy of attention.

Lee also delivered a sensitive performance of the first three Chopin Nocturnes, op. 9.

A piano quartet composed of Patti Lee, Mrs. Pearl's son Adam on violin, Thaddeus Collier on cello, and Sarah Kim on viola, played the andante movement from the Piano Quartet in C Minor, op. 60, by Johannes Brahms. The group gave a cohesive interpretation of this mournful movement. Especially captivating was Collier's fine cello playing.

Following a brief pause, Victor and Adam Pearl played *Vocalise*, by Sergei Rachmaninoff, and the Sonata in A Major by César Franck. Both these works contain strong melodic lines that were elegantly executed.

The thoughtfully organized program, along with excellent musicianship, provided a fitting send-off to a mainstay of the classical music establishment. Adele Pearl will be missed in Philadelphia and around the world.

Victor didn't hesitate. The review deserved a place in Adele's concert album. This, then, and not her obituary, would be the final entry.

PART IV

Sound waves don't ever go away... The wave simply expands, infinitely. The sound remains.

—Alexander Chee, *Edinburgh*

34

Adam sat on the passenger side of Thaddeus's VW bug with his violin snug between his knees. Thaddeus's cello took up the back seat. They were driving up the New Jersey Turnpike for a rehearsal; they were playing first violin and cello in the Mendelssohn Octet at the Ninety-Second Street Y in a couple of weeks.

"What's with you today, Pearl?" Thaddeus said. He was too big for the driver's seat. "Giving me the silent treatment? We left almost an hour ago, and you haven't said more than three words. You could at least read off the names of the service stations; they're so euphonic."

Adam laughed. "Sorry, I'm distracted."

"I'm an ear if you want, friend."

Why not? "I thought I'd feel better after we got through the memorial concert, but I admit to feeling crappy," Adam said. "Spotted one! James Fenimore Cooper Service Station!"

"That's the spirit! Considering those service stations are for tanking up, taking a leak, and loading up on junk food, they've got some fancy names. Now, what about the crappy?"

"I've lost my footing," Adam said. "Actually, I wonder if I ever had any footing to begin with."

"Sounds harsh." Thaddeus swerved right to let a tractor-trailer leaning on his horn pass. "Take it from me, you have plenty of reason not to be fine right now."

"Let's start with Hissle," Adam said. "I got twisted up about him for no reason."

"Piece of work, isn't he? They say he had a thing for your mother."

"I've only just realized that."

"All your years at Caldwell and you never heard that before?"

"Nope."

"Maybe the rumors passed you by because you're her son. Were her son. Are her son. Oh hell. I'm not helping."

"You think there's any way he and my mother kept up?"

"You mean an affair? No way," Thaddeus said. "Hissle's deadwood. He landed in the back of the section a long time ago, baby. Your mother dumped him, and he never got over it."

"Hissle basically said that to me at the memorial concert," Adam said. "Said Adele 'had a way of being friendly and cheerful that cut you out.' He's still burned up about it."

"My point exactly," Thaddeus said, opening his window to give the finger to a pickup truck that had just zoomed past. "Goddamn Jersey drivers." He changed lanes again. "Something's eating at you. Maybe you don't need to hold on to it."

"True." Adam wondered whether misery was a crutch. He watched cars stream by. The giant gasoline storage tanks outside of Newark were coming into view, accompanied by a nauseating, sulfurous smell. "But then why did my mother...?"

"Spit it out, Pearl."

"When I was going through my mother's papers, I found this love note from Hissle. If you could call it that. He had a screwed-up way of expressing affection."

"Are you surprised?"

"Not by that, but by the fact that my mother kept it."

Thaddeus thumped the steering wheel and let out a loud guffaw. "Ha, ha, ha. C'mon, Pearl! We know Adele had a first-class ego. So she kept Hissle's little love note. Who wouldn't? She wasn't the kind to say no to flattery."

"You must be right." There was virtually no possibility that Adele had had an affair with Hissle during her marriage. Victor and Adele spent much of the year together on the road, and when they were home, they were rarely out of each other's company unless they were practicing or teaching a few studios down from each other at Caldwell. They adored each other, which Adam had always known.

"Okay, forget about the phantom affair," Adam said, recalibrating. "Here's a horrible admission: I get what Hissle was saying. I'm afraid I feel—felt—the same way."

"What way?"

"I sound like an angsty twelve-year-old," Adam said. "But like Hissle, I often felt I was just another obligation of my mother's, like she treated me with the same good cheer and friendliness as everyone else. It's not that she shouldn't be upbeat, it's that as her kid you crave real connection. Hissle said he couldn't get underneath her famous good cheer. It was the same for me. My mother didn't let down her guard, not even for me, her son. Maybe for my father, but not for me." He thought about Victor, tapping into Adele's love to power him forward. Thank goodness she'd left Victor what he needed.

"I hate this emotional excavation," Adam went on. "But it's the truth. I'll be goddamned if Hissle turns out to be the one to call out what's eating me."

"Pearl, in this life, help can come from unexpected sources," Thaddeus said. "I've learned that much. You're in mourning, I get it. The world reorders itself and makes you deal with your shit. Avoiding it is worse.

"For what it's worth," Thaddeus continued, "when my father died, I had to go to ground. Get in touch with people who knew me and him when I was a kid, reconnect to people with shared memories. I'm from upstate New York. Dad was our Little League coach. He cut the old ladies' lawns in the neighborhood and made us do it too. Smacked me around but good. Didn't think I was manly enough. Hated the damn cello, thought it was for sissies. I never got a dime from him once I left home. He didn't give a shit how many tables I waited. He was about pulling yourself up by your bootstraps. He came around eventually—sort of—showed up at my Caldwell graduation recital and said the music was pretty. Thank Christ Caldwell was free, or I'd probably be pumping gas in Schenectady."

He took both hands off the steering wheel and held them up in front of the windshield.

Adam reached for the wheel, but Thaddeus grabbed it first. "Actually, I could have been a welder. Lotta guys from my high school ended up as welders. Think I'm tough enough?" He took his right hand off the wheel for Adam to feel his muscle.

"Sure thing, Thaddeus. Would it be possible to watch the road?"

"I would have made more money welding than playing cello."

"Wish you had?"

"Naw. I chose music. I had to work hard to get here, figure out how to make a living. For all the bullshit, I wouldn't want it any other way."

"That's nice," Adam said, thinking how different it was for him. Music had chosen him, or been chosen for him, a natural outcome of his upbringing, which had been rich in many of the ways that Thaddeus's had not. Adam's Paris jaunt had proved that abandoning his violin was a poor choice, like removing an essential part of his diet. Adele had proposed Paris; she set Adam on the path to realizing that his violin mattered to him.

"What do you mean by 'going to ground'?" Adam said.

"Losing a parent is a life-changer," Thaddeus said. "I needed to reconnect with my crowd, even if I hadn't talked to them in decades. Needed to swap stories, remember the great things about my dad."

Adam thought that "going to ground" might also mean Dara. Dara's flight had left a cavity that reopened after Adele died.

"So, your mother didn't love you up," Thaddeus said. "I'm not minimizing that; it hurts like hell. But that was a long time ago. Maybe you're ready to move on. Adele is gone, and there's not a bloody thing you can do about it." He shifted into high gear and roared past a UPS truck. "How the hell can they deliver packages if they drive so slow?

"If I'd held on to every one of my father's whacks, I'd still be cowering in a corner," Thaddeus continued. "I've got my own son now. All I can do is try not to beat the crap out of him. Let him find what sings to him instead of what I think he should do. And believe me," he said, leaning over to Adam, "you don't know the number of days I'd love to give him a swat and tell him to respect his old man. But Francie would divorce me. She's a softie, she's got the whole mommy thing going. Speaking of which, do you think we'll make it back by eight tonight? I try really hard to tuck my kid in."

"Only if we double the tempos in the first movement," Adam said.

35

Where are you off to, car keys and all?" Yvette said, as Dara grabbed her purse and buttoned her coat.

"Cecil Rothstein finally agreed to sit down with me. He promised we could meet before I interview him on campus at the end of the month. Can you come to our gig?"

"Of course I'm coming. The signs are plastered all over campus."

Dara smiled. "It's hard teaching a course that's cross-listed between the English and the music composition departments. I hope it'll be interesting. We've billed him as the 'quintessential American classical composer.' He's eighty-nine and emeritus here. Lives in Bryn Mawr. His compositions went from atonal to tonal. That's unusual."

"Stoked for your event, aren't you?" Yvette said with a grin.

"Yeah! They sent invitations to the whole English department, and the music department too." Dara checked her watch. "Have to run before he changes his mind."

"What's the connection to English?"

"It's his concept of time. He thinks like a writer. Well, he is a writer, a musical writer, and he also writes books. His philosophy of time connects to Virginia Woolf. Oh, and *Penn Magazine* wants to do a profile of him as renowned emeritus faculty, so I'm writing an article for them too."

"You're on a roll, girl."

"Come in." Cecil Rothstein's housekeeper led Dara through the dimly lit front hall to his living room. He had a head crowned in white, a beard and mustache to match, and a face that suggested a life of trials.

Rothstein looked up from his armchair and folded the newspaper. His gold-rimmed half glasses slid down the edge of his nose. "Hello there, young lady."

"It's been a long time since someone referred to me that way," Dara said, certain he would miss the irony. He was dwarfed by a Steinway grand covered with sheet music and staff paper, and hemmed in by books and sheet music stacked around the floor. Dara stepped over the piles and slipped into a chair in front of him.

"Anything interesting in the paper, Mr. Rothstein?"

"Same bad news. I read it anyway, especially the obituaries. At my age I usually know someone. You wait. You'll be the same way."

"I just went to Adele Pearl's memorial concert. You must have known her."

Rothstein nodded. "She was on me for years to write a piece for two pianos. I called it *Fire Duo*. She and Victor premiered it at Carnegie Hall. It was in the early seventies, I think. I had some quibbles with their interpretation; they took it too slow in the andante movement. But it was well received. They recorded it a year or two later if I recall." He waved a gnarled finger toward a stack of CDs. "If you look, you'll find it there."

Dara started to get up. "Don't bother," he said. "We're not putting any music on now. I can't even hear with the stereo off. Find it in your music library. What was it you wanted?"

She reached into her briefcase and pulled out a small tape recorder. "Do you mind?"

"Do I have a choice?"

Dara smiled and clicked on the machine. "What happened to move you away from atonality?"

"I got a lot less popular; I can tell you that. You try bucking the establishment! You rub their faces in the mud by saying the famous guys are writing drivel that no one can sing or play, let alone listen to! You make it clear their work sounds like fog-horns in the middle of Broad Street. It's not a way to make friends or curry favor with the musical powers that be."

"I guess not," Dara said. "Are you referring to innovation?"

"What's innovation for innovation's sake? I hate that term! It makes for empty music." He glared at her. "What about craft? If you care about it, they slam you for being 'derivative.' What are we, if not derivative? You're going to tell me Mozart didn't listen to Haydn? Or Brahms to Beethoven? What kind of cockamamie garbage is that? Cultural elites don't know their frying pans from their tuning forks."

"I was expecting something different," Dara said, pulling her chair closer to his. "I know you endured a devastating personal tragedy," she continued, referring to his late teenage son. She was concerned her question would darken his mood but needed to verify whether this loss had prompted his stylistic U-turn.

His pursed lips made it clear she'd overstepped.

"Adele wasn't like you," Rothstein said, as if they had spent the whole time talking about the Pearls and he hadn't just unloosed a tirade against twentieth-century music. "Adele was serious all right, but she wasn't interested in studying. Not like you, eh? You sent all those notes pestering me for more reading. Article this, book that. I did see your emails," he said, pushing up his glasses, "although I hate the computer."

"I'm known for being persistent," Dara said.

"I can see why," Rothstein said. "Adele was about the score. Victor is a different story. He's read my books. Used to visit me in my studio at Penn to talk things over. Deep intellect, that Victor. I wonder how he's coping. It's not easy losing a spouse." Rothstein's voice quavered.

"I once knew the Pearls' son," Dara ventured.

"You asked about my son," Rothstein said. "George, his name was. Killed at age seventeen by a hit-and-run driver on Market Street." Rothstein's glasses fogged. "Don't you dare tell me he shouldn't have been out at three a.m.! Plenty of people are out then and don't die."

"That's so—"

"You never get over it," Rothstein said. "I was a different

person afterward. I refused to write anything to please anyone. I did it my way, public be damned. And," he said, leaning precariously forward, "I'll tell you a secret. My music improved. My compositions became more authentic, closer to the soul." He sat back and shut his eyes. "You never get to where you want to go, you just keep pushing the rock up the mountain."

Minutes went by. Dara thought Rothstein had fallen asleep. He sat up with a jerk. "Stick to your guns," he said. "Don't be persuaded by what some phantom critic thinks you should do. Be true to yourself."

"I will, Mr. Rothstein," Dara said soberly, realizing he'd just delivered essential wisdom.

"Did you say you know Adam Pearl?" Rothstein asked.

"Knew him," she said.

"Excellent violinist. Can you imagine having Adele for a mother? She must have been one tough cookie." Dara thought of the music saturating Adam's home. In hindsight, she saw she'd undervalued her own mother—a woman with a sense of humor who was warm and generous, even during Dara's split with Matthew—and that she'd overvalued Adam's. Maybe Adam had suffered having a mother like Adele; maybe that suffering had given him depth. Adam hadn't expressed it that way, he wouldn't have; they'd been too young.

"What did you say your business was today?" Rothstein asked.

"We're interested in your theory of time, Mr. Rothstein. That's what I want to focus on in our campus interview."

He was quiet.

"I teach a seminar called 'Time, Music, and the Twentieth-Century Novel,'" Dara said, trying to elicit a response. "You're an expert on time, aren't you?"

"I've dog-eared some pages," Rothstein said, bending forward to choose a book from a stack on the floor. She hoped he wouldn't tip over. "I expect you'll have your students read my work."

Rothstein's writing was opaque; she would never impose it on her students. "For purposes of the campus interview, I'd suggest you describe your theory from scratch," she said. It was going to be a bear keeping him on track for their presentation.

"The point is," he said, leafing through the beat-up paperback he'd just retrieved, "there isn't an obvious succession to the way we live our lives. Time moves forward, but our lives unfold without a plan, unforeseeable and unpredictable. We're forced to sort the events of our lives, otherwise the past takes over and we lose our ability to prioritize our present."

Dara thought about this. She'd calibrated time through books. Not what was assigned for class, but what she curled up with late at night or crammed into the corners of her day. Sophomore year she'd inhaled Walker Percy; junior year, May Sarton. Deconstructionism would have finished her off without the magic of *One Hundred Years of Solitude*; time stopped when she discovered Zora Neale Hurston's *Their Eyes Were Watching God*. Hadn't *Crime and Punishment* opened a conversation with Adam at Briarly?

"It's about form and order," Rothstein said.

Dara regrouped. It wasn't books that calibrated time, it was music. Music—the good and the bad—had opened her to everything that came after. Her first meeting with Adam, *Finlandia*'s brass plunging her in sound; the concert at Briarly where she was enveloped in the Brahms Piano Quintet, twice. Adam and music were inseparable. She still couldn't listen to some of the pieces they'd heard together for fear of the memories they evoked.

"Is this what you're after?" Rothstein asked.

"Yes," Dara said. "The more you can elaborate, the better."

"About musical repetition," Rothstein said. "It should have the same impact that memory does in life. The past telescopes into the present." He shut the book. "It's all in here, young lady. Speaking of time, I'm not interested in wasting mine," he said, dismissing her.

"Thanks so much," Dara said, standing up to pick her way through the piles. "We're looking forward to your presentation."

"Let's hope I live that long," he said. "At my age, I don't buy green bananas."

Dara approached the on-ramp to the Schuylkill Expressway. Trucks and buses lumbered by, blaring horns and belching out diesel fumes. She craned left to get over, then changed her mind and stayed in the slower lane. It was nice to feel like a graduate student again; she liked contemplating the meaning of meaning. She hoped she could elicit Rothstein's brilliance in public. He wasn't an easy subject; he was ornery as hell. His losses gave him a wariness of the past, as if it were a place too treacherous to tread.

36

To: Professor Dara Kingsley
        Department of English
        University of Pennsylvania

Dear Dara,

If the woman I saw jogging away from the Independence Theatre was you, thank you for coming to my mother's memorial
concert. Any interest in catching up over lunch?

Yours,
Adam

37

"Victor, I need your help!" Dieter Brendt backed Victor against the wall in the hallway at Caldwell. "The most magnificent song cycle ever written, and it's up to you to make it happen! Please. My accompanist dislocated his shoulder, and my recital is in three weeks." Brendt's German accent made him sound more desperate. "Schubert's *Die Winterreise*, of course you know it."

Victor wished Brendt would let go of his lapel. "When is it again?"

"Three weeks from today."

Victor needed Brendt to retreat. But he couldn't muster the strength to decline, although he'd assumed the memorial concert would be his last public appearance. Taking the score Brendt thrust at him, Victor said, "I guess I can give it a whirl."

It had been years since Victor had heard the *Winterreise*. Before practicing, he decided to read the poetry that Schubert set to song. He pulled a volume off the wall and sat down in his green easy chair. Wilhelm Müller's dark verses bewailed unrequited love. Songs filled with ice and snow, grief and longing, hopelessness and despair. It wasn't just the poet who was despondent, it was the composer as well. Schubert made his final notations to the *Winterreise* on his deathbed, and breathed immortality into Müller's words.

Victor leafed through the score. He wasn't sure the poetry was award winning, but the music was. Songs followed one upon another, each melody more pointed than the previous, the finished whole a masterpiece of twenty-four songs.

Victor stood and turned on the lamp next to his piano. *Die Winterreise* was a duet. The piano set the tone, rhythm, and tempo for each song. For close to forty years Victor had not played a duet with anyone except his wife—and son.

He opened his keyboard and read through the first few lines. Adele waved across his piano lid, her voice carrying over the music. *Pick it up, Victor, don't let the tempo lag or Brendt will run out of breath.*

Victor stood up and looked at the piano bench opposite. Empty.

He sat down and started into the first song once more. Adele's eagle eye checked his feet. *More soft pedal, Victor. For heaven's sake, don't make Brendt strain to be heard.* Brendt wasn't even here! Neither was Adele.

Victor didn't know whether to laugh or cry. He should never have accepted this assignment. He closed the score and turned off the lamp. Since he had no choice—he had to learn his part—he put on his coat and headed back to Caldwell, hoping the piano in his studio took up enough space to crowd out ghosts.

At Caldwell, Victor couldn't dwell on his broken heart; his preparation time was too truncated. Even if he'd wanted to, he wouldn't have managed. Dieter Brendt came by regularly to assess progress and badger him about their rehearsal schedule.

They practiced on the small stage in the Caldwell Concert Hall, Brendt's clear baritone ringing against the fruitwood paneling, the room empty except for a few admiring students peeking through the great wooden doors.

"Victor," Brendt said, "I like that you don't play like a soloist. No crash and bang; you're a great listener!"

"I was trained by the best," Victor said, eyes tearing.

38

"Tell me again why you're turning down lunch?" Lily asked over the phone.

"It's not right," Dara said, pacing her living room.

"What's wrong with it?"

"I'm the one who ditched him."

"Maybe you've grown up since then. You appear to be a functioning adult. You have a fancy career. Plus, there's zero chance that Adam has been waiting around for you for twenty years."

Dara laughed. "How are your parents?"

"We're taking my mother to the neurologist on Monday. It won't be pretty. She can't remember what city she lives in. My dad's acting like he can handle everything, which he can't. I have to get them more help. God knows where the money's going to come from."

"Jesus, Lily, how do you do it all? Do you have any time to play?"

"Wanna hear something nice?"

"Please."

"I'm accompanying Lucy Choi in a recital at Mannes. She's on their violin faculty."

"Love that! What are you playing?"

"A new sonata she commissioned by a Danish composer she met in Spoleto. Also Beethoven. Maybe she'll get a critic to come."

"Lily, that's so exciting! Promise you'll tell me when it is? I'm coming up for it."

"Lucy's good. You'll like her sound."

"Can't wait." Dara sat down on her sofa and sighed. "Adam looked damned good at the memorial concert. But I can't see him or anyone else right now."

"Who's seeing anyone? He's probably married with six kids."

"Good point."

"I could get all mushy and say the stars have aligned for you," Lily said. "That your paths are supposed to cross again."

"You think so?"

"How the hell do I know? Sometimes there's a reason for these things. Don't wait for the Second Coming. And tell him I say hi."

39

Adam decided to walk to West Philly to meet Dara; it was a biting, sunny day. Would he shake her hand? Give her a hug?

"Adam!"

She was standing in her forest-green coat outside Judy's Café, playing with the end of her braid, the way she used to.

He didn't hesitate. She felt familiar in his embrace. "Didn't mean to bang you with my violin; I'm coming from rehearsal."

"No problem," she said.

They walked through the café to one of the back rooms. Dara sat down in her coat. "Adam, I meant to write you a condolence note; I should have. I read your mother's obituary in the *Inquirer*," she said breathlessly.

Adam tucked his violin under the table. "No need for a condolence note."

A waitress handed them menus. "Water?"

Dara unbuttoned her coat and tried to hang it on the inside of her chair without standing. "It's nice to see you," she said, readjusting her position so she could sit on her coat. "That's better." She looked up. "Someday I'll invest in a ski jacket. It would be easier." She sounded as if she'd picked up with Adam after a day or two apart. "It must be hard for you," she said, more slowly.

The waitress reappeared.

"Could I have a minute?" Adam said. He couldn't tell if he was asking the waitress or Dara, who had skipped any small talk. Dara ordered tomato soup. "Tuna on croissant," he said, not particularly partial to tuna.

"Is it okay that I'm asking you about your mom?" Dara asked, now fully focused on him. She had crow's-feet when she smiled. Her eyes had lost some of their sparkle. Adam saw a sadness that hadn't been there before.

"Of course! No one else has."

"How can that be?" Dara said. Silver would overtake chestnut in her long braid, still thick, hanging across her left shoulder. "What is wrong with everybody?" she said, as if demanding a reboot of Adam's past few months.

"No one wants to talk about death," Adam said, realizing this anew. "Crazy, right? We're all going to die." She nodded. "It *is* hard," Adam said, returning to her earlier comment, "though not necessarily in ways I expected."

"What were you expecting?" Dara said.

"Well, you know your mother has a terminal illness, so you're forced to think about it. Or not."

"That's called denial," Dara said.

How much of his past few months had been about denial? And how much of his life before that? "My mother wouldn't even tell me she had cancer," he said. "She left that to my father." He recalled his yearning to crawl under Adele's soundboard and sleep away her news.

"Oh, Adam," Dara said, placing her right hand over her chest. "That's heartbreaking. How is your father? I always liked him."

"Doing okay. He's accompanying Dieter Brendt in a recital next week. It's a big step forward for him."

"Your father is lucky to have you."

"I'm lucky to have him." Adam was unprepared for Dara's solicitude. "What do you remember about my mother?"

"It was bliss hearing her play," Dara said. "Remember her solo Bach concert?"

"You were in another world," Adam said, a world away himself, a time warp—savoring memories experienced alongside Dara before they passed into separate lives.

The waitress arrived with their orders.

"It was always music, music, music in your house," Dara said, peppering her tomato soup. "You were easy with it, born to the trade."

"That's not true!" Adam said, surprised at his vehemence. "It wasn't easy. I mean it was, given that it was all my parents talked about. But it got harder." He bit into his sandwich. Too much mayonnaise, always the problem with tuna. "What about you?" he said. "Your family?"

"My parents are fine," Dara said. "Touch wood. They downsized to an apartment in Haverford. They have their aches and pains but don't complain."

"Tell them I asked about them. If you're comfortable to."

"They really liked you," Dara said. Adam was having trouble navigating Dara's openness. Maybe she'd always been this way, but it was in stark contrast to anyone he'd spent time with recently. "Remember my annoying big brother?" Dara said. "He's a stockbroker. Got his act together and married a wonderful woman who's levelheaded and fun. They have three adorable little girls. My nieces. Seven, five, and three. They live in Merion."

"That's nice." What wasn't she saying? "You're married? And maybe you have children?"

"No kids. My marriage..." Dara stirred her soup. "Can we wait on that? I'm interviewing Cecil Rothstein in a campus lecture."

"The composer?"

"That one. Is there another? The English and music departments are sponsoring it. My course is cross-listed. They've put up posters all over campus." She looked pleased. "Anyway, Rothstein accused me of pestering him. Thinks I'm too persistent."

"That must be a compliment coming from him." Where was she going with this?

"In my field, I have to be tenacious, or I'd never publish anything." She looked at Adam. "Publication is the currency of academia. Regards from Lily," she said, abruptly changing the subject, again.

Something felt off. "How is Lily?"

"She's still wonderful, feisty Lily. Supports herself playing ballet lessons and performing a few times a year. She's playing with Lucy Choi, a new commission by a Danish composer. You would know who he is."

Adam nodded, drifting.

"I saw Hissle on the way to the reception at the memorial concert," Dara said.

"But you weren't at the reception. I looked for you."

"You did?"

"Yes."

"Wow," she said, gazing at him. "Anyway, Hissle didn't remember me... It worked out for the best," she added.

Adam looked at her. "What did?"

"I love what I do now," Dara said. "Your mother would be scandalized that I abandoned the viola." She put her hand over her mouth. "My timing is terrible."

"My mother is a mystery."

"I feel awful talking about this when you've just lost her."

He ran his fingers through his hair. "What was it about my mother?"

"I was intimidated. She was kind of formidable. At the same time, I thought of you as two sides of a coin; your personalities, at least then, were different, but you shared a lot too," Dara said.

"Heads or tails," Adam said vaguely.

"Adam, I can't imagine why you wanted to get together today."

"Idle curiosity," he said, smiling. "Nothing better to do."

She laughed. "I have to teach this afternoon." She stood up.

"Now?" he said, standing as well.

"Unfortunately. Well, no, I like teaching." She touched his forearm and looked at him as if she had more to say, then reached into her purse and left some money on the table. "Thanks for suggesting this. It was great," she said, leaning forward to kiss his cheek. And hurried out.

40

For the second time within a few short weeks, Dara found herself leaving Adam Pearl. She was late for her seminar, "Time, Music, and the Twentieth-Century Novel."

She hurried toward class. Adam was very good-looking. Better up close than at the concert. His hairline had receded. His eyes were the same shade of warm. He was wearing a heather-green crewneck sweater over a white shirt and tie. He should have ditched the tie.

All the things she hadn't said—that she loved his recordings (she owned them all), that he played like Orpheus at the memorial concert.

That she loved him.

Did she?

She had just sat across a table from him.

Hissle was a bad nightmare, ancient history.

Adam was deep; Matthew, two-dimensional. One a symphony, the other the lead singer in a band performing in front of a mirror. Even allowing for youthful ignorance and panic, Dara had missed her cues with Adam.

Adam walked down Walnut Street, struggling to make sense of lunch. Dara had seemed fidgety and nervous. She'd questioned him as if it were her right. He hadn't expected her attentiveness. In their short encounter, she'd demanded more of him than anyone else had. (He hadn't given Patti that chance.)

Words poured out of Dara like a fountaining dictionary. But had she actually said anything? He still didn't know the reason for her flight so many years ago. It seemed like a bridge she wouldn't cross. There must have been someone else in her life. Adam hadn't considered this possibility at the time, but he should have. College boys. Maybe he didn't want to know; he wanted his vision of Dara to remain untainted.

He stopped to watch the Schuylkill River meander through the city. It was forever ago that he'd practiced in his bedroom as Dara studied, that he'd been pressed against her in his narrow bed, rapturous.

She had a husband, whom she'd declined to discuss.

Dara knew him when. She seemed to understand where he was coming from.

Adam turned south on Eighteenth Street and walked toward Caldwell. He thought of the warmth and pliancy of her skin. She'd had a way of softening after they made love, the skin on her back less taut, as if she'd released the stress she carried. He remembered that, despite all that came after.

Dara had challenged him with the unfamiliar. Once she had signaled optimism and, he'd thought, love.

Breathless, Dara threw open the door to her seminar room, the last to arrive. "Sorry," she wheezed. She dug into her brief-case. "While I'm getting organized, I want to remind you that I expect you all to attend the presentation by Cecil Rothstein. I'll be interviewing him. We'll cover the material we're going over today from a different perspective.

"Now, let's get your thoughts on *Orlando*," Dara said. "What's Virginia Woolf doing with time here?"

Jessica raised her hand. "I like the way Virginia Woolf de-constructs gender, as well as time."

"Gender is key, but let's hear more about time," Dara said.

"Here's a passage I marked," Jessica said, thumbing through her book. "'An hour, once it lodges in the queer element of the human spirit, may be stretched to fifty or a hundred times its clock length; on the other hand, an hour may be accurately represented on the timepiece of the mind by one second.'"

"You missed the best part," Eliza interrupted. "Woolf says when a man reaches thirty, his thinking becomes 'inordinately long.' He starts asking, 'What is love? What friendship? What truth?' His whole past rushed 'into the falling second, swelled it a dozen times its natural size, coloured it all the tints of the rainbow and filled it with all the odds and ends in the universe.'"

"What role does memory have here?" Dara asked. She had not permitted herself memory, not after Adam, not after the Matt debacle. She'd kept to her books; they didn't hurt when everything else did.

Jessica and Eliza were engaged in a heated argument. About what, Dara had no idea.

Melt in his arms, that's what I'd like to do, she thought. His long fingers calloused from decades of violin playing. What it felt like when he hugged me this afternoon.

What happened to my resolve to make the most of single-hood?

What resolve?

I don't even know him.

I feel like I've known him forever.

Three students were waving their hands in the air.

"Yes, Miles?" Dara wondered where the discussion had gone.

That wretched, hot, rainy Philadelphia afternoon.

Maybe Adam was the reason I failed at marriage. He left a long shadow. Forget the other boyfriends. They were stupid, mostly. Drew turned out to be gay (he was nice, actually). Cal was a narcissist (like Matthew, now that I think about it). Let's not go into the one-night stands, too much inebriation. I figured if I studied enough, I'd live happily ever after. With Matthew.

Adam unlocked the door to his Caldwell studio. In a routine more familiar than breathing, he opened his case, removed his violin from its blue silk bag, and rosined his bow. Closing his eyes, he drew a down-bow across his violin's lowest note and began a long, slow G major scale. He flexed his left hand around the neck of his instrument to stretch his fingers. His G string vibrated in a wakening rumble. This was his church, his temple to peace and concentration. He put his overworked thoughts aside and focused on the instrument in his embrace.

His left index finger planed an A, up-bow expertly placed between bridge and fingerboard. Gradually, luxuriantly, he ascended to B and then C, drilling in his fourth finger for D.

The veins in his hands swelled from warmth. Up, up, up he traveled, shifting to third and then fifth positions on the E string, climbing to the apex of the scale. He played long tones, his mood lifting with the pitch. He basked in sonorities ricocheting around his studio, filling his body from belly to skull, his sound an exaltation to hard work and to music itself.

Three octaves—twenty-one notes—meticulously laid, lavished with care on his violin. His instrument was an extension of himself. Relaxed and nourished, he descended the scale with exactitude, pausing over Dara's comment that he and Adele were "two sides of a coin."

He wondered if that was true.

Adele's side was a hard-driving, single-minded quest for perfection. By contrast, Adam's musical life was not a destination but a journey that anchored him through years of disappointment and frustrations in love. It was solace and exhilaration.

More than an exhortation to interpret the music, Adele had given Adam his center. No matter what crowded his emotional life, he could pick up his violin to find equilibrium. His mother was the source. He felt a surge of appreciation for Adele Hammond Pearl. And saw that Dara had delivered him here.

41

Psst." Yvette stuck her head out of her office. "Come here."

Dara sat down in the chair facing Yvette's desk. Half of Yvette's head had turned royal blue over the weekend. "Excellent," Dara said.

"What?"

"You're an inspiration. Watch out, someday I'll shave my head or go platinum blond or both."

"Bring it on! Guess what I have?" She pulled a square of paper from her top drawer. "It's Babycakes!" She shoved the sonogram across her desk to Dara.

Dara couldn't make out anything beyond blurry stripes on a page. "So exciting!" she said

"We heard the heartbeat! It thumps and swishes around the room when Carmen has her checkup. That's our baby!" Yvette said, returning the paper to her desk drawer.

"That has to be the most thrilling thing in the world."

"It is."

"How's Carmen doing?"

"She's fine, she keeps saying she feels like Mother Earth," Yvette said, grinning. "You didn't ask how about me! I'm getting her cravings—Thai food—especially pad thai with tofu, coffee ice cream, and warm, soft pretzels. With French's mustard, of course."

"Amazing," Dara said.

"For the record, Dara, are you planning to take off your coat and stay a while?"

"Oh yeah," Dara said, realizing she was still dressed for the outside, and clasping her briefcase like precious cargo. "Do you have another minute?" Dara stood up to extricate herself from her cold weather gear.

Yvette looked at her watch. "I'll give you one, then I have to run."

"I just had lunch with him."

"With the ex-prick? I thought we were steering clear of him."

"We are," Dara said. "We definitely are. No, Adam. Did I tell you his name when we talked?"

"Wait a minute! You mean boy wonder? Adonis of the violin?"

"Stop! I'm trying to be serious."

"Well, excuuuuuse me! I thought you hadn't seen him in twenty years! This is the one with the dead mother, right?"

"Correct, great memory."

"Very funny."

"I went to the concert he and his father gave to honor his mother."

"And you didn't tell me? When was this?"

"Last month."

"Let me guess, you rushed up to the stage door afterward and sank into his arms?"

"Will you cut it out?" Dara was laughing so hard she was crying. "Apparently, he saw me hightailing it out of there and got in touch."

"He was the one who got in touch? The plot thickens."

"It seems he hasn't forgotten me." She started to cry in earnest. "I didn't tell him anything. I should have." Yvette pushed a box of Kleenex toward her. "I should have said something about the ex-prick and about why I left Adam."

"Get real, Dara. It was lunch, not a confessional. Besides, what's to confess? I hate that idea. Were you supposed to deliver a summation of the last two decades? You weren't in a lecture hall, Professor."

"I appear to be finding my inner ocean," Dara said, tears streaming down her face.

"It's called having feelings," Yvette said.

Dara sniffled. "I guess."

Yvette stood up. "Feelings mean something. You gotta go with them." She started collecting books and papers.

"That's what scares me," Dara said.

42

Adam stopped by his father's studio at Caldwell. "Guess who I had lunch with yesterday?"

Victor shrugged.

"Dara Kingsley."

"The viola player?"

Adam nodded, surprised by his father's quick recall.

"That breakup was hard on you."

"You remember?"

"How could I forget? I'm your father, for Pete's sake. I tried to get Mother to make it up to you."

"How?" Adam couldn't imagine his parents discussing that kind of thing.

"Mother knew she was off; she knew her knee had jerked the wrong way."

"I don't think so," Adam said. "I agree that Mother was off. But she meant what she said. That's how she was." Adam did not want to relitigate that horrible night. It was a long time ago. He was not interested in reenacting the whiny schoolboy, nor did he want to injure his father. Adele was dead. Silenced.

"I'm sorry you remember it," Victor said.

"It was kind of unforgettable," Adam said, regretting wading into this discussion, and acutely aware that his mother was anything but silenced.

"Adele was extraordinary in so many ways. But apologizing was not her strong suit," Victor said.

"You can't apologize for telling the truth, Dad." Was Adam defending Adele? "Mother was nothing if not direct."

"True." Victor looked pensive. "All I can say is, she knew she was wrong. She was terrified of impairing her relationship with you. She was worried she'd done damage."

"I wonder why she didn't say so," Adam said, putting up his hand to stop Victor's response. "I know. I just told you that Mother couldn't have apologized. She didn't have it in her. I'm not making sense. Seems to be the norm nowadays."

"I understand. Believe me," Victor said, smiling sadly. "What's Dara up to?"

"She's an English professor at Penn." She sounded like one, Adam thought. Inquisitive, brainy. "I've known where she was, but I never bothered to look her up."

"And?"

"She's married."

"Oh."

"She came to the concert. Mother's memorial. I saw her running up Walnut Street."

"You didn't say anything."

"What was I going to say in the middle of that crowd?" Adam had an uncomfortable memory of Patti at his side as they reentered the theatre for the reception. "I asked her out to lunch."

"Ah." Victor nodded thoughtfully. "And obviously she accepted."

"Yeah."

"I always liked her," Victor said. "You were good together."

Adam was disconcerted to find himself choking up.

43

To: Adam Pearl
From: Professor Dara Kingsley
Re: Condolence Note

Dear Adam,

I hope belated is better than never. I am so sorry for the loss of your mother. Having the chance to listen to her up close was a great gift.

Your mother not only leaves a huge hole in your life, but also a lot of unanswered questions. A wise mentor once told me that you can continue to get to know your parents even after they're gone. I wonder if that will be the case for you. After all, you're a man who asks a lot of questions and knows how to think. I believe your understanding of her will broaden and deepen as you get older.

I wish I had sent this note earlier, but since our lunch, I really wanted to get it down on paper (meaning email).

Love, Dara

44

When did they split up exactly? Victor left Caldwell and walked back to his apartment. Adam had been a student. Yes, that was the reason he moved to Paris. Adele had suggested that he get away from it all. Give the boy a change of scenery, in Paris no less. Pearl and Pearl had played two concerts in Lyons that year.

The girl must have made an impression. Had Adam been carrying a torch for Dara all these years? Victor felt slow not to have realized this.

What an awful conversation Victor had had with Adele that night. "Words are like musical notes," she'd said, sighing. "You can't carry them around; the minute you play them they're gone. They're dispersed once they're uttered. They're shadows in front of a bright light."

What should Victor have done? He'd been useless for the pale comfort he'd tried to provide.

Adam wasn't hiding how much he still cared for Dara. Victor was pleased they'd met up again. Maybe Dara was the reason Adam hadn't been able to settle down. Victor wished that boy every happiness. Lord knew he deserved it. His son, whom he loved without boundary, who had watched over him through his grief. Who had visited each day, gentle and attentive, never overbearing. Who shared Victor's pain but could soothe as well.

Victor unlocked his apartment, hung up his coat, and bid his usual hello. "Yes, dear, I would like some tea. And, yes, I'll get to your things."

He found a garbage bag under the kitchen cabinet and, teacup in hand, walked back to his bedroom, determined to complete his latest project, emptying Adele's dresser. He'd made his first foray into it the week before and retreated in haste. Her bureau was radioactive. He'd started too late and knew he wouldn't sleep if he continued. This afternoon, he would push through.

Adele's sweater drawer smelled like her—perfume as recognizable as her morning scales. Soft cashmeres lay one on top of another, folded and ordered in a rainbow of colors. Bella would know what to do with those. Victor removed and stacked them on the bed without disturbing their order.

He opened Adele's top drawer: underwear, bras, and stockings. Underwear and bras were easy. He would throw them down the building garbage chute so he wouldn't have to see them at the bottom of his kitchen trash. He picked up the bag he'd brought in and started tossing in her undergarments.

Wait! They were Adele's; she had worn them! His dead wife's warm body had filled these things. It was sacrilege to throw them out, and a misery to keep them. Just a few months ago she had lived in them and now they would be relegated to a dumpster.

What was a life worth?

He moved to the right side of the drawer and fingered her stockings. These were worse. Adele purchased hosiery in small boutiques in European capitals. She washed her stockings by hand in whatever hotel rooms Pearl and Pearl found themselves. Couldn't someone use them? Maybe Bella would have an idea. No! Adele would hate that. They were hers, privately and lovingly hers. Victor would have to dispose of them. In one motion, he scooped them up and threw them into the garbage bag. "Please don't judge me, Adele," he said.

The top drawer was finished. Victor sighed with relief. He started to close it, then saw it wasn't quite emptied. There was one last item, a handkerchief with his initials embroidered in blue. *VDP*, for Victor David Pearl. It was from their Carnegie Hall debut, their formal entrée into the world as Pearl and Pearl. Victor had brought it onstage to clean the keys between movements, as he did every concert. Adele had asked him for it in the Green Room. She said she wanted to keep it always, a memento of the birth of their team.

Victor held it up to his cheek and smiled ruefully, simultaneously honored and flattered that she'd kept it all these years.

"I'll keep it, dear," he said, sliding it into the top drawer of his bureau. "Forever."

He was shattered anew.

45

What was Dara trying to say in that email?

Adam couldn't figure out how to answer it.

He decided to go to her lecture on Cecil Rothstein instead.

Adam was pretty sure his parents had recorded Rothstein's *Fire Duo*, but he'd never listened to it. There were plenty of Pearl and Pearl's recordings Adam hadn't listened to. He needed to live his own life. He wasn't responsible for knowing his parents' entire output.

46

S o," Dara said, leaning into the lectern to conclude her introduction. "We're here to explore the elasticity of time." It was almost three thirty, and she had taken too long, though the afternoon had gotten off to a late start. She scanned the audience. The hall was packed, several hundred people, students and some faculty. It was too dark to see anyone, except Yvette grinning from the middle of the front row, bless her.

"We experience life in the present, but the present is fragile," Dara said. A week had gone by, and she hadn't heard from Adam. Maybe she shouldn't have sent the email. "The past has a way of hijacking the present," she said. "That's what Mr. Rothstein will discuss today.

"I'm not speaking of historical past, which is also critically important. I'm talking about our past and present as individuals. Past and present combine in ways we can't control. We know the past can hold trauma, but it may also hold love and comfort. It can hold intimacies that have been lost forever or simply misplaced. In short, the past gives the present meaning, and thus gives meaning to time."

She had thought she and Adam had rekindled a long-dormant connection. But it must not have been mutual.

"Time is not only a preoccupation for writers, but also for composers," Dara said. "We're fortunate to have Cecil Rothstein with us today, a celebrated musician and composer who's taught generations of students at Penn.

"But first," Dara said, putting her aside her notes, "a digression."

Enough. If she couldn't say it to Adam, she would speak to the assembled students. It was time to unburden herself.

"When I was your age, I was working toward a career as a

professional musician. Viola was my instrument. My great love
of music is one reason why I admire Mr. Rothstein's work. But
music became a source of agony for me when one of my teachers made it clear in very cruel ways that I should abandon the
viola for lack of talent. He called me 'deaf,'" she said, tripping
over the word, "which is a poor attribute for a musician, as you
might imagine.

"We could spend the rest of this lecture on shame—my
shame—but that's the notion I want to dispel. I experienced
these admonishments as epic failure, as the end of everything
I knew. And in many ways, it *was* the end of everything I knew.

"But here's where the healing properties of time come
in. Eventually, I arrived at a different opinion. We weave the
various strands of our lives as we live them. All of it matters:
the good, the bad, and the indifferent. We need failure in our
journey; it's a critical vehicle for learning."

Why had Dara waited so long? Telling her experience to an
audience of students was easier than she'd anticipated. Maybe
they would learn something from it.

"Now to the heart of the conversation," Dara said. Rothstein had better be in a good mood, she thought, or he, too,
risked going off script. "Mr. Rothstein's music is performed
around the world for a reason." She walked to Rothstein's chair
and bent to adjust the microphone clipped to his jacket.

He was still awake, a promising sign.

47

As the crowd filed out, Adam walked to the back of the lecture hall, unsure what to do with himself. Dara was surrounded by well-wishers and earnest-looking students.

Dara had been like an acrobat spinning plates at the podium. Her theories about past and present (whose past and present?) were riveting. She was able to make Rothstein's ideas comprehensible, a minor miracle since Rothstein was so obtuse. And she was married. Adam wondered if he was here out of a morbid compulsion to have his heart broken all over again.

Whatever precaution he felt, Adam was also mesmerized. He had been in a full-blown fantasy—admiring Dara's authenticity in such an intimidating setting; delighting at how she braided musical experience with professional expertise; thinking how sexy it was that she was smart, how he'd known brains were sexy as long as he'd known her, which felt like for forever even though they'd had no contact for decades—until Dara launched into that tangent. Dara's comments jolted him out of his musings. There could be no doubt she was referring to Phillip Hissle. It wasn't necessary for her to name him.

How had Adam missed the role that that man played in Dara's life? Adam thought he'd put Hissle to bed once and for all. Now what?

He'd just decided to slip out and consider these questions in the cold light of reason, when Dara pulled away from the knot of people surrounding her and waved.

❧

"Adam! I can't believe you're here. I didn't see you. Thanks for coming. I didn't expect you to come. Can we get away?" Dara said, hurrying Adam outdoors.

She was trying to take in that he'd heard her lecture. What exactly had she said? It was if she'd conjured him. Which was impossible. "How's this?" She swung open the door to Center City Java. "I may be able to reclaim some anonymity from students here."

She ordered an espresso. "Adam, do you even drink coffee?" She didn't know anything about him, suddenly.

"I'm okay with hot chocolate," he said.

They found a booth in the back.

"Dara," Adam said. "What's going on?"

"Did you get my email?" She was too keyed up to think straight.

"I couldn't figure out how to answer it. I'm not a writer. To be honest, I'm not big on email. I figured I'd show up instead."

"Oh. I thought... Well, you didn't answer, so I was about to give up."

"Give up what?"

"You'd think I would have had enough time to come up with a coherent narrative," Dara said. "Hissle did say I was deaf." She pushed on with no idea what Adam was thinking. "Repeatedly. Muttered sotto voce insults. And Isaac was gone. Hissle didn't say much—he didn't have to—it was enough to blot out all of Isaac's goodness." She looked at Adam. "This is so yesterday."

"Time has a way of compressing," he said. "I just heard a lecture about that."

"Very funny," Dara said, afraid she was going to cry. "It was crushing. I couldn't continue. Only I never told you, I just left. I couldn't bear the thought of you finding out, or your mother for that matter. I assumed you'd never speak to me again if you knew."

"Dara! Slow down, please," Adam said, raising his hand. "This is kind of big."

"It ruined my life for a while," Dara said.

"It wasn't great for me either."

"I know that. I really do." She wanted to apologize but remembered Yvette's advice. Prostrating herself felt wrong.

"Somehow, I knew tenacity was not going to get me anywhere in music," she said. "I wasn't going to be able to power through. So that part was okay, even though at the time it felt like defeat. I was miserable about it, in fact. But I did need to cut loose from music. The problem was you."

"Me?"

"Well, you weren't the problem, only I figured you were, because of what you represented."

"I didn't represent anything!"

"I know," she said again. "Believe me, I definitely figured that out."

"I had a rough time," he said, hesitating. She didn't want to hear what came next. "I never cared what you played or even if you played at all. It left a huge hole, your leaving as you did."

"Warped youthful reasoning," Dara said, a tear sliding down her cheek. "You learn things in hindsight." She looked at him. "Or when someone you've injured has the generosity to sit down with you." She laid her hand on his. "Thanks, Adam. I mean, for being here, for giving me this chance. I made a huge mistake, throwing out such a good thing with you." She shook her head. "I figured you had talent, admirers, you'd be fine."

"It wasn't like that," Adam said. He looked at her with an expression that was hard to read—sorrow, compassion, anger? "I feel terrible," he said.

Plaintive, that's what it was. "You're not the one who should feel terrible," Dara said.

"I should have realized," he said.

"How could you? I never said anything," Dara said. "I tried really hard to hide it, in fact." She was done hiding things; it only meant tying yourself up in knots.

"I wish you hadn't." Adam spoke quietly. "It's taken me years to understand that things that are second nature to me come at huge cost for others. I guess I can thank my family for that. I work hard, but I'm not in pitched warfare with myself when I practice."

"That's what I'm saying," Dara said.

"Still, I had a tin ear; I wasn't paying attention."

"I had other things going for me," Dara said, ignoring his comments, "but not that. I had no more music left in me. That's you," she said. "Music. I had words. A lot of them. And that turned out to be a good thing."

"I have a rehearsal," Adam said, pushing back his chair. "I wish I didn't."

"Adam, I don't think we're finished this conversation... I mean, I have more to say."

"Well, then, I'm all ears."

"What works for you?"

"You could come to my dad's concert next week. I want to make sure he has an audience, if you're okay with that. Catch a drink afterward?" He stood to go. "Dara, you were the best thing..."

48

"My mother has early-stage Alzheimer's." Lily sounded resigned over the phone. "Not a surprise. But it sucks big-time."

"That's terrible! How'd your dad take it?" Dara said.

"He's Mister Cheerful. I guess that's better than being morose."

"I guess. What can I do for you?"

"You can answer your phone when I call. Where the hell have you been?"

"Hiding."

"From me? What gives?"

"It's Adam," Dara said. "Unfortunately."

"Only you could think that was unfortunate."

"I think he's some combination of furious and confused."

"So, you had the Hissle conversation."

"Sort of. Adam showed up by surprise to my Rothstein lecture, and I ended up talking about my little Hissle debacle to the crowd."

"You're kidding."

"I didn't even know Adam was there. It just came out, as if I were talking to my younger self, as if she were sitting with the students in the audience."

"But instead, you ended up talking to Adam."

"It wasn't my plan—I didn't know he was there—but that's what happened. I wanted to tell those students, especially the young women, not to be afraid, to prize defeats and learn from them."

"You're supposed to be over that bastard Hissle by now."

"I guess I am." How diminished Hissle had been at Adele's memorial concert. That was what Dara had been trying to disentangle in front of her audience.

"Just remember, you were one victim among many. You got picked for his weekly torture. Consider it an honor."

"Is it weird that it's easier to address a crowd than to say these things one-on-one?"

"That's something artists have been doing since the dawn of time," Lily said.

"Wow, Lils, that's profound. I'll have to chew on that."

"How'd you leave it with Adam?"

"No clue."

49

From the left side of the Caldwell Concert Hall, Adam could see his father's hands on the keyboard. He no longer needed to choose between sitting right or left. His mother's absence loomed; how much more it must loom for his father.

Dara had come early and suggested she sit in the back. Something about not being able to see Victor right now.

The performers walked onstage—Dieter in front, Victor hanging back for the singer to acknowledge the applause.

Adam was overjoyed to see Victor performing. In the depths of his grief, Victor possessed an admirable certainty. His love for Adele was unencumbered by doubt. To Adam, it was an elegant simplicity.

Dara seemed intent to focus on…what? Adele? Hissle? Her work? Adam couldn't tell. Why was she so rushed, words pouring out of her as if she'd been stoppered up for years? He kept turning over her comment that she'd made a huge mistake. He was overcome with sorrow for the irretrievably lost, for their having sailed past each other. Should he have gotten in touch earlier? He couldn't have; he'd been too summarily dismissed. He had been that self-protective. But to what end?

Victor adjusted his piano bench, and they began. Victor was in control, his playing restrained and elegant. It was a pleasure to watch him.

Brendt strutted back and forth. His voice was crystal clear. He was a showman. Victor stayed in the background, attuned to singer and song.

Adam immersed himself in Schubert. Victor was a fine musician, beaten down by months of caring for his ailing wife, flattened by her death, yet brilliantly managing this performance.

Die Winterreise wound down. Victor exhaled; his shoulders relaxed. He removed his feet from the pedals and dropped his hands from the keyboard. With a burst of applause, the concert ended. Victor rose from his piano bench, and Dieter reached for his hand for bows.

Victor was brave to take on this performance. Adam was afraid Victor would break down if he acknowledged it, so he stood behind people offering congratulations, relishing their praise of his father.

"Pearl!" Thaddeus said, coming up from behind. "Nice job on your dad's part."

"Right?" Adam said.

"What'd I tell you? He's doing just fine. Time for a drink?"

"Can't. I have a date, sort of."

"I like the sound of that." Thaddeus barreled out.

Dieter thumped Victor on the back. "You rescued the concert! It wouldn't have happened without you."

"You sang like a nightingale," Victor said.

"Congratulations, Dad," Adam said, giving Victor a hug.

"I'm glad you came."

"Wouldn't have missed it for the world."

50

Back in his apartment, Victor switched on the light and hung his overcoat in the hall closet. The living room was quiet and dark.

Turning on a few more lights, he walked into the kitchen and put up the kettle. "Yes, Adele, I would like a cup of tea," he said, the corners of his mouth creasing into a smile.

It was agonizing, but it could be done. There was an untapped world of sonatas for every instrument in the orchestra; there were lieder for singers. They all required piano accompaniment. Victor was hardly ready to rush forward, but he could see the possibilities.

He just wouldn't be able to practice at home.

51

"Wine?" Adam asked, after he and Dara were seated at Philly Pheast on Twentieth Street.

"I'd love a glass of red. Share a plate of hummus?" Dara put down the menu. "Your dad played beautifully," she said. "It was kind of emotional, seeing him without your mom."

"It was." Everything felt emotional nowadays. "I wasn't sure he'd make it. But he's a pro," Adam said, savoring Victor's performance.

"It was weird being in the Caldwell Concert Hall. I don't think I've been there since...I was with you."

"That was a long time ago," Adam said. "Dara, tell me about your life now."

"I have a great job," she said, as the server delivered drinks. "Cheers," she said, clinking her wine glass with his. "To...reunions."

"To reunions."

"I can't believe I get paid to study and teach," Dara continued. "But I have a feeling that's not what you're asking."

Adam felt himself coloring.

"I think you're asking about my marriage," she said quietly. "I won't be soon, I hope. Married, I mean."

"Excuse me?"

She took a sip of wine. "It's not like the way I left you. Nothing like that." She laughed and wiped away a tear. "Despite my eagerness to interrogate you, I haven't figured out how to talk about my issues. My husband was running around. My ex, I mean. I was a fool. I'm not supposed to get this upset talking about it. But with you, I feel ashamed."

"Ashamed?" Dara getting divorced? What should he do now? His first reaction was to get up, take her in his arms, and swing her around the dining room.

"It's pretty sordid, actually," Dara said, weeping.

Adam was struggling to take in this new information. He took a clean, pressed handkerchief from his back pocket and handed it to her.

"Thanks," she said, dabbing her eyes. "I should take a vow of celibacy. I think about it, you know."

"You can't be serious!"

"It's been bad," she said. "I thought I had it all figured out. I couldn't have been more wrong."

"Do we ever have it figured out?" Adam didn't know how to comfort her, or what comfort would look like. Maybe this was what all her rushing was about. "I hate that anyone would treat you like that."

She broke off a corner of pita and dipped it in hummus. "I'm learning in the school of hard knocks."

"We all go to that school."

"I suppose. What about you?"

"What about me?" Had she closed the subject on herself? "Lots of relationships strewn by the wayside. Some more successful than others. Some were so lonely it was painful."

"Meaning what?"

"I'm trying to figure it out," Adam said. "Something about my mother's death has forced me to look at things."

"Ah." Dara sniffed and looked pensive. "She had her opinions."

"She didn't keep them to herself. Often I didn't agree, especially when it came to people."

"She wasn't nuts about me."

"Let's not go there. She and I fought about it, believe me." He didn't want his anger rekindled. He wanted to stay present. "My mother was incapable of imagining a life beyond music. And that's being generous. Music mattered to her more than hearth and home. More than me," he added, wondering if he still believed that.

"I'm a little stunned that you're getting divorced," he said.

"Sorry to be insensitive. I don't seem capable of filtering anything."

Dara dabbed her eyes and smiled.

"My mother judged people within her musical hierarchy, including whoever I was dating. I only dated musicians after you, I'm embarrassed to say."

Madame Cliquot floated through his mind, and then away again.

52

Victor wandered into the living room. He ran his hand over the lid of his piano, afraid to open his keyboard, let alone Adele's. Yet here he was, planning to go to Aspen. Alone. As a lovely coincidence, he'd learned that Brendt would be in Aspen at the same time.

He sat in his green armchair and stared at the two pianos, quiet as death. You had to continue growing your whole life, like it or not.

He was curious about his master class. Each summer there was one student whose talent jumped out. Someone to cultivate and encourage, on whom Adele could bestow enthusiastic career guidance. Victor was the spotter, who said "That's the one." The one whom critics would praise five years hence as the latest musical sensation. Adele honored Victor's endorsements, eager to involve herself with another young musician.

He dreaded the new round of condolences from people in Aspen who hadn't made it to Philadelphia for the memorial, or who might not have heard that Adele had died. The ones who couldn't put pen to paper or preferred to save their comments for seeing him in person.

53

I thought you'd end up with a musician," Dara said, sipping her wine.

"I hope not," Adam said, too quickly. "Based on my experience, it seems like a bad idea. Although it would be great to be with someone who understands music, who knows where the drive comes from. You can't explain that to people."

"No, you can't."

"I don't have a great track record," Adam said. "My mother got excited about a couple of girlfriends, but I ignored her. I had to. What do I care if they play in the Philadelphia Orchestra? After you, I stopped arguing. There was no point. I wasn't going to let my mother choose a partner for me.

"Somewhere along the way I think I shut down," he added.

"I guess your mother's passing triggers old injuries," Dara said.

"Like what?"

"It feels like she wasn't there for you in some fundamental ways," Dara said hesitantly. "I'm sure she loved you. In fact, it was obvious she adored you. You don't make those kinds of demands on your son if you don't. But she was caught up in the sparkle and lift of her life—what a life she had!—and maybe you got lost in the shuffle. That can make for loneliness."

"You said so at the time."

"I did?"

"It stuck with me," Adam said, arrested before a glaring—and, in the instant, obvious—truth. His mother had not been there for him. Puzzle pieces fell into place. "I wonder if that's the real source of my grief," he said, more to himself than Dara. Whatever was unavailable from Adele prefigured the mixed-up fog he'd been in since her death. "I've felt a kind of grief ever since I can remember," Adam said, naming it for the first time. It was his longing to hide beneath his mother's soundboard. The spreading vacancy he felt when he left Patti's the last time; the theme and variations he'd replayed with a parade of women. The bass obbligato that was his life's accompaniment.

"That makes me sad," Dara said.

"Don't be." Adele was dead, and Adam would never get what he wanted from her. That was reality. Thaddeus had tried to tell him that. "Somewhere, I've always known this," Adam said, both stricken and relieved.

"Are you okay?" Dara asked.

He nodded. "Can you stay a little longer?"

"For you, I'll consider it," Dara said, "even though I have a dozen papers to read tonight, with musical accompaniment. I have a habit of doing my students' assignments to make sure I'm being reasonable. I had them work in pairs. The English students are working with the music composition students."

"Nice," Adam said.

54

It wasn't getting any easier, but Victor was getting better at it. He'd become more indulgent of people's efforts to console him. Rather than asking how he was doing, they clutched his hands, recounting their difficulty in accepting Adele's death, or how his bereavement reminded them of their own losses. No one looked Victor straight in the eye and said, "What a hero you are to get up every morning; it's incredible that you manage to put jam on toast with your heart ripped out."

Even that wasn't quite right. It was more like, "What a miracle that you're here, with fifty percent of you gone. Is there any music left in you? Did your ears slam shut when she died? How do you manage to smile?"

But Victor could, he did smile. As his loss sank deeper, his smile became broader. What a life he'd led! Duo-piano literature adorned his living room, a secret world he'd learned to decode. The dazzling places he and Adele had visited, the stages they'd graced. Each piano was a new experience, a challenge to play to its best advantage. Pearl and Pearl.

Adele had kept up with dozens and dozens of people, but it was Victor to whom she gave the keys to her private self. He knew all of her—the sparkling pianist, the passionate lover. Mother to their beloved son. The imperfect, excitable, excited woman whom it had been Victor's privilege to partner.

55

Tell me more about what you study, what gets you up in the morning," Adam said.

"Besides coffee?" Dara dipped a carrot in hummus. "I'm a Victorian lit specialist, but that's generic. I'm expanding into the twentieth century and thinking about Virginia Woolf. She plays with time. She can write a whole novel that takes place in one day or skip decades with the simple phrase 'Time passes.'

"To a certain extent, all fiction writers play with time," Dara continued. "They have to. A book is a finite object in space, whereas time is infinite… Stop me, or I'll go on forever."

Her excitement was palpable, infectious.

"Music takes place in time and is ruled by time— Jesus, I sound like Cecil Rothstein. Time signatures are the first things we learn as music students. They order our hearing, dictate the rhythm. On the other hand, where is the actual music? We can't touch it or feel it.

"Well, we can feel it," she said, eyes filling. "You did that."

"What?"

"I listen to your recordings. I have them all. I listen to them except when they make me cry."

"Dara!" He reached across the table and squeezed her hand. "You're so…"

"Where was I? I got myself distracted." She thought for a moment. "Oh yes. Since you can't see or touch music—"

"I never think about the theoretical stuff," Adam said.

She looked up at the clock on the wall. "Adam, I hate to do this, but it's getting late, and I have to grade papers and do my own assignment." She started to get up. "Where do we go from here?"

Adam stood and said, "I once knew this wonderful girl. I don't think I ever got over her." He helped her on with her coat. "I was afraid to think about her—in fact, I avoided thinking about her for years—because it ended too soon and too abruptly."

"Why would she do a thing like that?" Dara said.

Adam shrugged. "Beats me."

"Don't make me cry again."

He scooped her up in an embrace. "How are you getting home?"

"I was thinking of walking," she said.

56

Adele," Victor said aloud, "I'm glad you went first. I hate the thought of you struggling through this." Adele could not have tolerated a life without Victor. Victor knew it, even if she hadn't. He had been the foundation from which she spread her wings, confident she would return to safety.

It was silly to play out this scenario. Victor permitted himself because it helped organize his life, cleaved by Adele's death. He used to live in Time Before. Now, he lived in Time After. He could stoke his memory to inform his future, whatever it held.

57

A dam and Dara walked west on Walnut Street. A light snow was falling, streetlights illuminating the flakes. Adam wrapped his arm around Dara. She leaned into him. They walked in silence.

Adam wondered if they could continue the night together but saw that Dara needed time. Her husband had inflicted damage. Adam didn't want to exacerbate her pain and didn't want to scare her off.

"I'd ask you in," Dara said, when they reached her stoop, "but I have a stack of papers waiting for me."

Adam looked at her, her hair white with snowflakes, her cheeks flushed from cold. He held her face. "I'll wander the streets," he said, and pointed to his head. "There's a lot going on up here."

Dara nodded. "I understand."

"Good night, Dara." He leaned over, brushed the flakes off her hair, drew her close, and kissed her.

"Do we get a second chance in this life?" Dara said.

"That's more than I know," Adam said, running the back of his hand down her cheek. "Sleep well, Dara."

"Sleep well, Adam."

58

Dara made a cup of instant coffee and sat down at her desk. It was late, and the snow had muffled the city.

She picked up a sharpened pencil to try her students' assignment. She'd paired the English majors with the musicians and instructed them to write something together, inspired by Rothstein's talk.

Dara was neither poet nor lyricist, and she wasn't paired with anyone to set her words to music. Could she even do this assignment?

Adam settled into a bench in Rittenhouse Square and stretched his legs.

A layer of fine, new snow highlighted the tree branches. Buildings were dusted white.

Billy, the little bronze goat, shone.

Oh hell, Dara thought. There's no way I'll get this done tonight.

What were words without music anyway?

Adam stood up and brushed the snow off his head and arms.

Time to go home.

His cell phone rang.

Well, maybe not quite yet.

59

Together in her living room, Adam and Dara glowed in the light of the snowy night, the burgundies and blues of her carpet vibrating with the covers of her books. Dara had not had a lover in her house. Not here, the place that marked the end of her marriage, that saluted her independence, that even on her darkest days held the possibility of a fresh start.

"Dara, let me look at you."

"Adam—"

"Shh." He put his index finger over her lips and drew her to him, the softness of their mouths against each other, the slowness of their tongues suggesting not only that they would take their time, but that they had captured time.

Adam laid Dara's braid over her breast, unclipped her barrette, and, plait by plait, undid her hair so that it spread loosely around her.

She was wearing a beige cardigan over a white blouse, her standard. Adam unbuttoned her sweater, his lips at the base of her neck, his cheek against the softness of her blouse. Her clothes, which until now had struck her as utilitarian, took on the gossamer feel of a ballerina's tunic.

"Come," was what she could manage.

She took Adam's hand to go upstairs to her bedroom. As she leaned over to pick up the books strewn across her mattress, Adam slipped off her sweater and blouse from behind. Setting down an armful of paperbacks, she turned to him.

She had to feel him against her; she had to undress him.

Her urgency left her winded.

60

Time stands still.

Having fled music, Dara is enveloped in song. She hears symphonies lush with strings.

Words have led Adam to the rhyme. Why spend all those years looking for love in places where the pitch was off? Love turns out to be where he started.

They stretch out on Dara's bed, naked and expectant.

Adam sinks into Dara. Her chestnut hair, her uplifted breasts.

Her pleasure in his biceps, her breath on his forearm. A kiss on each fingertip to honor the music within. She lays her hand across his belly and moves it sideways, then up and down, reprising the contours of his body.

He caresses her smooth legs, the bend of her hips. The curve of her abdomen, the taste of her bosom. He writes on her neck and inscribes her collarbones.

She perches on his thigh, arches her back. Strums his shoulders, listens to his beating heart.

They play a duet to celebrate love's return.

The music is in the rests.

Adam and Dara, flesh against flesh, heart to heart.

Stirred, lyrical.

Home.

AUTHOR'S NOTE

On October 27, 2004, I opened the *New York Times* to discover that Lilian Kallir had died. The obituary noted that she was a pianist "known for her elegant Mozart performances, both as a soloist and in duet recitals with her husband, the pianist Claude Frank... Her daughter, the violinist Pamela Frank, said the cause was ovarian cancer."

I had no connection to Lilian Kallir, except to have heard her magnificent piano playing when I was a young music student. In addition to mourning her passing, I was struck by the impact on her husband and musical partner who had lost not only his wife but also a significant part of his musical career.

Thus, the germ of a novel.

Isaac Koroff, the viola teacher in my novel, is modeled on a teacher of tremendous significance in my life, Max Aronoff, to whom I dedicate *Duet for One*. I fell in love with the viola and with music when I began studying with Max, who taught me three life lessons: (1) The music is in the rests; (2) if you break things into component parts, you'll figure out how to put together the whole; and (3) practice, practice, practice. I have never heard a sound comparable to what came from Max's viola, either before or since.

Max was in the first graduating class at Philadelphia's Curtis Institute of Music, a pinnacle of music conservatories around the world, due to its free tuition and outstanding faculty. Max was also a founder of the Curtis String Quartet. Readers of *Duet for One* may find some similarities between Curtis and the fictional Caldwell Institute of Music. I did not attend Curtis. Caldwell grew out of my imagination.

One of Max's many gifts to the musical world was his founding of the New School of Music, where I had my lessons. In my time, the New School was housed in a former mansion at Twenty-First and Spruce Streets in Philadelphia. The school no longer exists but was an important musical fixture for many decades.

The stories that Isaac tells in *Duet for One* came from those that Max told. Reba Aronoff, Max's wonderful life partner, is the model for Mrs. Koroff, including the stories she tells.

The New School of Music had its own orchestra, in which I was privileged to play during high school. Our conductor was the late William Smith, then the Associate Conductor of the Philadelphia Orchestra. Smith, a brilliant educator and musician, inspired the character of Charles Jones. I was lucky to play under him at Temple University's Ambler Music Festival for successive summers as well.

Finally, the character of Cecil Rothstein is inspired by the Philadelphia-based composer George Rochberg. Rochberg's book, *The Aesthetics of Survival*, helped frame Cecil Rothstein's conversation with the fictional Professor Dara Kingsley.

ACKNOWLEDGMENTS

I am indebted to Editor-in-Chief Jaynie Royal and Managing Editor Pam Van Dyk, the extraordinary duo at Regal House Publishers, for giving *Duet for One* a home. It was a joy to work with these wonder women to bring my *Three Muses* into the world, and I am thrilled to work with them a second time. Thank you doesn't begin to express it. And for my publicity team, Lauren Cerand and Daniella Sinder, I couldn't have done it without you.

Duet for One had a twenty-year gestation. Friends and family have been generous readers along the way. It is an incredible gift to have someone read your novel in draft. To all of you, I express my deepest gratitude.

Thank you to Robert Adelson for spending an afternoon way back when, talking about his mother's two-piano team.

Due to the passage of time, I am likely missing some early readers and commentators. Please forgive me. At the risk of unintentionally omitting people, I am grateful to those who read and commented on early drafts: Lauren Abramo, Paul Dry, Hope Gleicher, Alex Hirsch, Dina Hirsch, Georgina Hirsch, Ruth (Tiny) Hoffman, Jessica Krash, Lisa Lang, Carolyn Lerner, Clara St. John Longstreth, Char Mollison, Alan Morrison, Anne Morrison, Rebecca Morrison, Lorrie Pallant, Stanley Pallant, Anthony Pipa, Molly Rauch, Peg Romanick, Karen Sagstetter, Rima Sirota, Lorin Stein, Jane Bowyer Stewart, Alex Tang, Charlotte Thurschwell, Emily Toll, Elizabeth Toll, Connie Toll, Mary Kay Zuravleff, and the late Zelda Edelson, Michael Loeb, Seymour Toll, and Deborah Visser.

As *Duet* has grown and matured, additional readers and editors have offered invaluable support and advice: Lila Becker, Naomi Becker, Michelle Brafman, Helena Campbell, Tanya Coke, Nadia Ghent, Naomi Goldstein, Ruth Goldway, Amy

Gottlieb, David Groff, Gwendolyn Mok, Ericka Taylor, Kathy Sommer, Jane Bowyer Stewart, and Michelle Wildgen.

Profound appreciation for the musicians with whom I had the privilege to perform chamber music in college: Scott Hempling, Robert Kapilow, Sharon Like, Jane Bowyer Stewart, and the late Benjamin Ward. To Helena Campbell and Suzanne Ornstein, thank you for being there when I had to face the music.

Throughout my life, I have been blessed with support and love from a constellation of amazing colleagues, friends, and family. Thank you from the bottom of my heart. To Jane Bowyer Stewart, for being there in every possible way, including as a brilliant editor and copy editor, my utmost gratitude. Any mistakes are mine. To the women who have had my back starting at age four—Cary Bricker, Rachel Cavell, Naomi Goldstein, Liz Kislik, Julie Langenberg, Nancy Liebermann, Gwendolyn Mok, and Kathy Sommer—I wouldn't be me without you.

My late father, Seymour Irving Toll, adored classical music and educated himself about it to an astonishing degree. My late mother, Jean Barth Toll, who regretted her parents' lack of interest in her early violin lessons, put tremendous effort into my musical education. I am eternally grateful to both.

To Lila, Naomi, and Dan Becker—you are a constant source of joy and amazement. Thank you for being you.